THE MOMENT

BLOOD BOWL

T0112764

THE MOMENT

BLOOD BOWL

DANIEL R. STEVENSON

TATE PUBLISHING
AND ENTERPRISES, LLC

Published by Tate Publishing & Enterprises, LLC
127 E. Trade Center Terrace | Mustang, Oklahoma 73064 USA
1.888.361.9473 | www.tatepublishing.com

Tate Publishing is committed to excellence in the publishing industry. The company reflects the philosophy established by the founders, based on Psalm 68:11,
"The Lord gave the word and great was the company of those who published it."

Book design copyright © 2015 by Tate Publishing, LLC. All rights reserved.
Cover design by Gian Philipp Rufin
Interior design by Mary Jean Archival

Published in the United States of America

ISBN: 978-1-63449-305-5
Fiction / Christian / Fantasy
14.12.01

Contents

Something Went Wrong

The day had become a sunny, few clouds kind of day. The heavy traffic and heavier traffic emissions cooperated to make the air feel like a heavy woolen blanket even in the lungs. It was that kind of day. Little sky was actually visible from the sidewalks of the city. Skyscrapers rose everywhere so that one's view looking up was glass and metal and maybe a hint of blue. It was that kind of city. He had spent the last eight hours combing the streets of the city, traveling from interview to interview, searching for a career in a city full of jobs. Long past tired, in the latter moments it had become a burning feet, like acid in your shoes kind of day. He pulled up next to the day care, cleared enough of the car seat for his son to find a place, and climbed wearily out of the car.

Seven interviews had yielded seven promises of additional interviews. During the traffic delayed journey back to the day care, three text messages scheduled the interviews for later in the week. Tomorrow would be a day for rest. He was looking forward to picking up his son and finding a hotel to relax for the remainder of the evening.

Little Buckaroos Day Care was filled with lights and sounds attractive to little minds. The huge glass entrance led to a lobby lined with clown statues, put there almost certainly to woo unsuspecting parents into becoming prospective clients and prospective clients into signing on the dotted line. The architecture interested Jeffrey. As an architect, everywhere Jeffrey went, he saw architecture and the questions it asked, the statements it made, and not least of all, the bills it paid.

Buddy came running when he spotted his dad. At four, Buddy was very affectionate but not so talkative. His mother had taken his voice with her when she had left home. She had joined a cult, and when Jeffrey hadn't followed her lead as near as he could figure, they had advised her that her eternal godhood was at stake (or some such), and that she must get out. She did and as far as Jeffrey could tell, had never looked back. She divorced him in record time, asking for nothing and surrendering full custody of Buddy with no more thought than one engages in while changing one's shoes.

"Get a job?" Buddy asked as the noises of the place invaded Jeffrey's mind and convinced him that no one who worked hard would want to come here every day after work. The whole thing had been arranged though, and there would be time to make better arrangements later.

"Not yet. Got some leads though," he answered. But Buddy was off fighting with some young girl for possession of a rocking horse.

"Leads are good…"

"Huh?" Jeffrey was caught off-guard. "Oh yeah, well, it's a start. Probably know something by the end of the week..."

Though Jeffrey had just been musing to himself about how adult conversation would be good, this woman was not what he had in mind. She busily kept her eye on the children. She seemed genuinely interested but more thoroughly distracted. Also, she had to be pushing sixty, with wrinkles where smooth skin had once been and pleasant smiles had turned the corners of her eyes into deep crevices peeking out from behind her twenty-years-ago-styled glasses.

In any case, she proved useful. She saved Buddy from the wrath of the little girl who had retrieved some blocks from a nearby table and was pelting Buddy with them out of dissatisfaction over the abrupt end of her turn on the horse.

Buddy was ushered up unaware of the impending trouble he faced from his dad. Jeffrey was too tired to lecture and really wanted to slip off to a nearby restaurant for a quiet meal or off to a hotel for a bath and a bed.

Buddy gripped his hand tightly and tugged him toward the big glass entrance. Jeffrey let himself be swept along. He fished for his car keys and started focusing on the exit. But he was stopped before he could slip away.

"Mr. Shaw," a man called after him. "Mr. Shaw, a moment."

Jeffrey stopped and turned and at the same time embraced a rising notion within himself that he was not going to escape so easily.

———◈———

Charlie exited the elevator and walked the short distance to the great double doors. He knew the path well, and he had agreed to meet his mother here instead of in the office or at her apartment to expedite matters.

He stopped at the large redwood doors and noticed the right door stood slightly ajar. She was already inside. Good. So far this was looking as if it would not take long.

"Charlie?" It was Mom. She was fixed up nice. Her hair had gone salt and pepper in the last months, but she would still be called beautiful by any man her age. She strolled into the main room from somewhere back in the apartment. "I'm so glad you came."

"It doesn't mean anything, Mother. I'm still undecided about this whole thing."

For six months, Charlie and his mother had been going rounds over the estate of Charlie's late father. Everything had been settled now except for one thing. Charlie's father had wanted him to have a share of the mansion. It sat pretty much in the center of the city, and everyone wanted the land. It would be easy to sell the mansion and divide up the profits. The problem—Charlie didn't want to give it up. Even though technically, Charlie's father hadn't left him a share in the will. Charlie had become the snag.

His mom and his two sisters had long since moved out. Gloria had taken an apartment while the old man was still alive. They were never much of a family, but Charlie's life was in the house, and he was not going to be pressured into giving it up, so some developer could come in and build a department store or worse, another skyscraper.

"At least listen, Charlie." She began putting her arm around his shoulders and directing him toward the center of a large room with a twenty-foot ceiling and an intricate mosaic on the floor. The room was cavernous with an overhead tiffany lamp for light dangling forty feet above.

"I'm listening, Mother. I'm just not sure what you can say." Charlie shuddered at the placement of her arm. She was not normally affectionate and had always been far too occupied with the bustling nightlife and politics of the city to pay any attention to him when he was growing up. *So,* he thought, *forgive me if I am not won over by your third attempt at showing affection ever!*

"This room was an ancient throne room," she said.

"Really?" Charlie was intrigued. He had been prepared for almost anything she might have said. She would probably not help him make up his mind today, but she had caught his attention.

He had been interested in this room since his father had purchased the building ten years ago. Something strange had nagged at him since his first visit. It was occupied then, serving as an apartment for a former mayor and his wife. They were aging, and the two had died peacefully in their sleep a few weeks back.

As a teen, Charlie had visited them several times exploring the winding rooms of this uniquely designed space. He had eventually settled into playing checkers with the old man, and in fact, old man Jackson had become more a mentor and maybe even a father to him than his own father during the most tumultuous years of his life.

"I know you've always loved this place, and when I found out a little of the history, I thought you would be interested," mother was still talking.

"What do you know?" he asked.

"Well," she began, "we are still waiting on some research but..."

Charlie strolled to where a one-foot dais ran the full length of the longest wall. It was four-foot wide and could have easily been a place where thrones once sat. In years past, it had somehow been covered by carpeting.

"As you know," she continued, "the building's original construction was almost two hundred years ago, back when monarchies were still common in many countries. It was the early days of the United Nations, and apparently, this room was considered foreign soil."

"So more like an embassy?" Charlie asked, running his hand along the wall.

"Maybe but there's more. Apparently, a king and maybe his queen were here in exile, and from here, the government helped them to mount a coup that resulted in their taking back control."

"What country?" Charlie asked as he squatted down and peered intently at a crack in the lower wall.

"We don't know, but a friend is trying to get that information. It was a long time ago."

"They'll probably never find out. History has concealed anything like what you are describing. So why…hello, what have we here?"

She came quickly to join him, and the two looked closely at a small bit of something like wick that ran in a crack up the wall. He gently pulled it upward, starting again every time it broke until it reached six feet above the dais's surface.

"What is it?" She asked.

"It actually looks something like oakum. Oakum was used in ships made of wood, made from old rope and tar or pitch or something. It was used to plug cracks between planks so that the ships would not sink."

"What?" She was amused but little more. To her, it looked like dirt and string. She wanted to steer the topic toward his consenting to the sale of the mansion. "Isn't this place full of interesting things?" she said lamely.

He gave up on chasing the wick higher and tried to follow the end of the groove near the floor, but it seemed to disappear under the mosaic. Then he saw something he had not seen before.

In the middle of the mosaic was a square that from the dais appeared to be a uniquely different color from the rest of the pattern. It appeared as if it had been patched at one time. Made of thirty-six identical smaller squares, it presented itself as an oddity. Nowhere else in the whole pattern could one find a square.

He went to stand near it and then reluctantly stopped. "Okay, Mother, why have you brought me here?"

"I want you to reconsider. Won't you please let me sell that old mansion? The girls and I have already done everything necessary, Charlie. Just a signature…"

"It's my home, Mother. Everything I have is there. I sign and then when someone does buy the place, I'm out. Anyway, Dad technically didn't leave it to me, so you can do whatever you want. Why don't you sell it to me?"

"I can't do that, Charlie. You know your father's dying wish and all. You can stay for awhile." She was pathetic. Her voice had the sound of pleading. It was a side of her he had not seen. "And then you can move here."

Ah, there it was, she wanted this place to entice him; and then now, his mind readjusted to consider the wick. It was actually too interesting, wasn't it?

"Nice try, Mother," He stomped down hard on the square and turned away. He stopped at the door, suddenly beset by an emotion that he hadn't felt in a long while. "Mother?"

"Yes, Charlie?" She sounded as if she was crying, but he dare not look back to see.

"I'll give you my final answer by Monday. But then, no more. If I decide to stay, I will buy you out and sign an agreement that if I ever sell, you still get your share. If I stay, you get nothing until then, agreed?"

"I suppose," she said, but there was relief in her voice.

After he left, she searched out the square in the floor. The small tiles of the mosaic had cracked under his heel. She broke her pen prying up the first piece, but after that, the rest came easily. In the small compartment below, she found an antique-looking bowl gilded in gold. It had to be worth something but not so much to her. She owned nicer things. She took it back to her apartment anyway, thinking how Charlie had seemed to think the whole thing was a trick, and maybe tomorrow she could convince him otherwise.

—⁂—

The man who had called him seemed somehow familiar. It took a second, and then Jeffrey remembered having seen him that morning when he had been dropping off Buddy, and a small bus outside had been spewing children. The face of the man was the face of the bus driver, but now he was in a suit and tie, and he seemed to have something urgent to say.

"What can I do for you?" Jeffrey asked, standing a little straighter and even recapturing a bit of lost energy.

"This morning, when you came in, you paid for the week with your credit card…"

"Yes." Jeffrey didn't like the sound of this and already began reaching for his wallet.

"Something went wrong with the machine, and we need you to step into the office so we can run it again," the bus driver said.

Jeffrey looked incredulous for sure. What's more, he had realized that his wallet was not in his pocket where he last remembered. *The wallet must be in the car,* he thought. He replayed the day in his mind, wondering where else he might have left it.

"That's odd," he told the little old bus driver, still trying to make things add up.

"Perhaps I should introduce myself," he said, "I am Jonas Buckaroo. This is my day care. I sometimes help out wherever needed."

"That makes sense," Jeffrey said out loud, not really meaning to but still somehow distracted by the missing wallet. "But I seem to have misplaced my wallet."

"Oh, that is unfortunate. Is there anything I can do to help?"

Hotel, Jeffrey thought. *No credit cards. No ID. This could turn into a real problem.* But he answered, "I must have left it in the car."

He turned and walked to the car, and searching the front seat, he found what he expected and nothing more. When he turned from the car and contemplated what he and Buddy were going to do next, he found Mr. Buckaroo standing right behind him.

"Perhaps, we can help with an advance and a place to stay for the night," Mr. Buckaroo said.

"That's very kind of you," Jeffrey answered. "Now we'll have to get to the bank right away in the morning and cancel cards and such. What a pain."

"What bank?"

"Common National They're everywhere. I saw several while I was running around today."

"We bank at Common National as well. In fact, one of the managers at our branch is a personal friend. I'll bet if I go there with you and vouch for your identity, it would help. Want to go now? Our branch is still open."

"I suppose. Why are you being so helpful? Isn't this going above and beyond the call?" Jeffrey pulled his keys from his pocket and moved to put Buddy in the car seat.

"Mr. Shaw, The clowns, the toys, and the lights—they are for the kids. But the people, they are for you. Besides, I told you, something went wrong with the machine."

At the bank, Jeffrey freed Buddy, opened the trunk, and pulled out his briefcase, reattaching it to his wrist. Its contents would be virtually useless without ID, but he couldn't risk them in the trunk for the time they would be in the bank.

"Hungry," Buddy said.

"When we're done at the bank, Buddy, sorry," Buddy buried his face in his dad's shoulder in that way he had of giving in and at the same time delivering a load of guilt. Jeffrey shrugged it off, and meeting Buckaroo at the revolving door, they entered the bank.

—◦◦◦—

Charlie mulled over the trick his mother had tried to play on him as he rode home in his limousine. The chauffer was a stranger as the regular man was on vacation. So with no one to talk to really, Charlie sat there, lonely. The one thing that was certain was that Mom would not have tried a trick like that except out of desperation, and even then, someone else thought it up.

It must have been Kelly. His sister Kelly was a devious socialite who had resented the loss of standing in social circles more than anything else when their father had died. Mom had offended enough people in high society that they were more than ready to ostracize all three ladies when dad's position and power were no longer a factor.

Now, for some reason, mom's determination seemed to grow daily—she wanted Charlie out of the mansion. Charlie wondered if something existed there that might be found resulting in her discomfort. Perhaps, she had a buyer already lined up, and the rest of her words were lies too.

Charlie had a brief yearning to call his younger sister Jackie and pour over the whole thing with her. Then again, she had signed the document too. She had said, not in so many words, that she was done. She had enough games. A week before, about the time she had signed the document, Jackie had moved into the apartment with Mom and Kelly. Charlie knew that she had a good-paying job and had been left a sizable sum, so the move wasn't precipitated by financial need. The three of them had always been tight, and he had often felt left out. So be it then. What's wrong with being alone anyway? He rode home—lonely.

Charlie's tireless search of the mansion had stretched over the previous three months. Still, nothing really interesting had turned up—secret passageways and hidden rooms—but nothing definitive about his father's mysterious past. This night, he had planned to continue searching the stables. Though they were mostly long relegated to disuse, he hoped almost beyond hope that they might hide something of interest.

House Guest and Stalling

Her name was Jackie, and her appearance was like a young professional. At this late hour, she had let her blouse slip out from her waistline, and she walked the marble floors of the gargantuan bank building in her stocking feet. Buckaroo had slipped away almost on the introduction, and Jeffrey was left to deal with the beautiful young brunette on his own.

If his mind had been on romance, he would have realized that she was interested, and that the absence of rings might indicate availability. However, his lost credit cards, ID, and other important details lured his mind away from romance to business. That was no small task, especially in her presence.

He was able to remember the account number of three of the four credit cards that had been lost, and that had impressed her. For her part, she had taken right to helping him upon the request of Mr. Buckaroo. She had made a number of phone calls on his behalf, requested a bank advance on his account, and had arranged for two of the four credit card companies to send replacement cards to the bank the next morning.

She had even fed Buddy pizza, which a delivery man had brought in not fifteen minutes after they had arrived. She had said that when Mr. Buckaroo had called ahead, she had immediately placed the order knowing that the boy would be hungry. This was a very thoughtful and charming young lady.

Buddy lay back, nestled his head into his father's shoulder, and before long, was asleep. His stomach was full of pizza, and his pockets were full of suckers. His dreams were full of pretty ladies, all of them were the mother of some other boy, and yet he slept the sleep of the dead, as little children often do. He would wake crying. Jeffrey and Buddy both knew that. He always did—since his mother had left. He was a sad little boy, but he still had one thing, and he clung to his father.

Jackie returned to her desk one last time and found that now both of them were sleeping. She put the envelope with the cash advance on the desk in front of Jeffrey. She was about to pick up the phone and make a hotel reservation when something stopped her. She suddenly felt the need to help them more. She had done all that the bank could have expected, but now she wanted to do something herself.

Forty minutes later, the three of them rode the elevator up from the basement parking garage and stepped out onto Jackie's floor. They entered the apartment, and Jeffrey met Gloria, Jackie's mom, and Kelly, Jackie's older sister.

The clock in the living room of the spacious flat showed 10 PM, and Jeffrey looked for where he could lay Buddy down. Jackie showed Jeffrey into a side room with a view overlooking Broadway twenty stories below. Jackie crossed the room to shut the floor length curtains and noticed that a bank of fog was obscuring the view of the mansion. Charlie would be there alone. A slight pang of sadness at the loss of her father, and then she turned to Jeffrey.

Jackie retrieved some blankets and a pillow from a linen wardrobe with pearl handles. She met Jeffrey next to the bed of a little boy, about six or seven years old, who slept soundly. There they made a bed on the floor and nestled Buddy into it.

"This is Jacob." Jackie brushed back the boy's hair and kissed him gently on the forehead. He did not stir.

"Yours?" Jeffrey asked. They were whispering though it was probably not necessary. They both knew the boys would not awake from talking.

"No, Kelly's but I do love him so."

"She doesn't look old enough."

"She is."

Again, a Jeffrey of dull wits and conflicting priorities missed the subtly competitive way in which Jackie spoke of her sister's age. He looked toward the door back to the living room of the fancy penthouse apartment and cleared his throat. They left the boys comfortably snuggled.

The stream felt so good running over aching muscles that Jeffrey did not want to climb out of the shower. Still, he had made for the shower not long after introductions and laying Buddy down. He didn't want to linger too long. The women would be waiting up for him. That was certain.

In the small living room, Gloria read a romance novel with her feet propped up under her. She had brushed out her long, naturally wavy, salt-and-pepper hair. She wore her make-up so subtly that no one would know it was there though it served to cover the slight effects of age.

Jackie half-reclined on the sofa. The light of her laptop screen gently bathed her face although the long days work had taken its toll, and her head slumped sideways. Her breathing became very gentle and even. She had only surfed for a few moments before nodding off.

Kelly leaned forward over her knees with the TV remote in her hand, watching the end of a TV show. She was riveted and thoroughly intended to grill Jackie about the man in their shower as soon as the show ended. She did not know that Jackie had nodded off and suspected that her mother was only waiting for the appropriate moment to grill Jackie as well.

—◦◦◦—

One stall left. After hours of searching, Charlie lay his suit jacket across a small wooden table and sat down on a stool next to the last stall door. The sign on the door read "Magick." The horse in the stall was actually Black. He had moved Black to the last stall when he had been about to search his stall three hours before.

After regaining his strength or at least his motivation, Charlie rose to his feet. He climbed the climb of a beat-up, old man to his feet and turned toward the stall. Up wasn't any more comfortable than the hard wooden stool had been, but he believed that beyond the goal of searching the entire stables lay his bed. So he slid the latch open and cracked the door. He swung it all the way open and dropped the rope to hold it there.

As he peered into the shadowy stall, Charlie found himself wondering how long it had been since a horse named Magick lived there. Their family had owned many horses when Charlie was a young boy. Long before waist-high weeds had taken over the south pasture, horse and jockey pairs had been common on the grounds. Now the track out back and the yard at the center of it were the only usable remnants of a bygone era.

He corrected himself. Of course, the stables would still be usable. Then he wondered whether he should buy more horses to keep Black company. Then he thought about how he had ruined his pants on this foolish endeavor. Then about how horses do not really fit in at a mansion in the middle of a huge metropolis. Then he thought about how it would be easier to ride a horse to get take-out food or pizza than to have the chauffer bring the car around. Then he thought about how anchovies don't go well on pizza, contemplated what if anything they do go well with, and suddenly discovered that his mind had wondered a bit.

Charlie shook his head to clear the unwanted wanderings and picked up the lantern from nearby. The lantern was kerosene or some such with a wick burning brightly at its center. The stables' fluorescent lighting consisted of one long row of fluorescent lamps installed down the center and wired to one switch. The lantern burned brightly enough to search one stall at a time. That left fearless Charlie standing in a two-hundred-year-old stable peering by lantern light into a stall that had belonged to a horse he had never known.

Charlie's eyes narrowed. His heart rate elevated, and his fatigue moved into temporarily forgotten status as he spotted something in the stall. He moved cautiously inward. The small space grew brighter as he carried the lantern forward. He sat the lantern down and gently fell to his knees. He clawed at a broken and loose wallboard to reveal more of what, if anything, lies behind. At the noise and invasion, Black backed the rest of the way out of the stall. Charlie's hopes and dreams edged forward from the realm of improbability to real potential as he pulled his find from the newly revealed secret compartment.

—◦◦◦—

Jackie rose slowly to her feet and looked at her mother and Kelly. Both had nodded off. Jeffrey had stepped into the room. He was clad in plaid pajama pants from the waist down, and his upper half was bare and still damp from the shower. He patted his gleaming, rough-cut pectorals dry as she watched.

Slowly, she felt herself pulled around the coffee table. She stepped gingerly, the carpet soft and warm under her bare feet. Their eyes locked on each other. She fingered the top button of her silk pajamas as she came near him.

Her heart raced as he pressed up against her. She felt self-confident and secure. He raised his hand to brush her hair back away from her face. She felt his breath on her tongue and the gentle brush of his lips on hers as he dropped the towel and abruptly pulled her close.

The Light

"Jackie," Kelly snapped. Jackie spun to see what Kelly wanted and awoke. The encounter had been so real that Jackie briefly closed her eyes, breathing a long sigh through her nose, but the dream was gone.

"What?" Jackie hissed.

"Sorry," Kelly said. "Anyway, we don't have much time. Tell us everything you know about this guy. No telling how long he'll be in there."

Jackie looked from Kelly to Gloria and back again. The TV was off. Gloria had put down her book and now held her drink with both hands. The expressions on their faces were of eagerness.

"I don't know," Jackie began. "I mean, he's divorced. He came here to find some work. He's had a bunch of leads already. He's…"

"What does he do?" Kelly asked.

"I think architect or something like that. He mentioned something in the car."

"How'd you get him?" Gloria asked.

"He came to the bank. He lost his wallet, and we were helping him get everything replaced. We gave him an advance, but I thought it would be a good idea to offer him to stay here. It seemed like the Christian thing to do."

"Right," Kelly said.

"You did well," Gloria said, and she bent over and picked up Jeffrey's briefcase that had apparently been moved near her while Jackie slept. Gloria swung the briefcase up on her lap and began working the lock.

At first, Jackie's jaw dropped, and then she quickly clicked the laptop shut and slid it onto the table. The rushed motion intended to get her to the case before her mother could open it worked against her. The laptop hit Kelly's drink, which spilt on some mail on the table, and on Kelly's toes, causing a gasp. In the same instant and less noticed, the bowl slid onto the floor.

Jackie apologized for the mess and still managed to get to her feet quickly. By the time she got her wits about her and reached the side of her mother's chair, the briefcase was open. Both women stared into the briefcase. Jackie's jaw dropped again.

—◦◦◦—

Jeffrey turned off the water and reached for the towel he had seen hanging above the toilet. His eyes clear, he stepped out into the steamy bathroom. Piled on the toilet seat were the pajama pants, T-shirt, and briefs he had pulled from his bag before getting in the shower. He noticed that a new toothbrush, a travel-sized toothpaste, and a comb sat up behind the faucet on the sink. *Convenient*, he thought, *considering I left mine in the car.*

He spent time while he finished his bathroom routine thinking of how thoughtful Jackie was. He was not in the market for a mother of his child, but if he had been, she would have topped the list from the short time he knew her. Finished, he sat on the toilet with the damp towel in his hands. He wasn't quite ready to face the women yet.

The hall clock chimed one time probably indicating 1 a.m. He threw the towel in the hamper, which was full. He pushed the wicker lid down only to find that evidently someone had already performed that maneuver, and the towel still kept the lid from shutting. He hung his head in his hands and debated how long he could hide in the bathroom before going out to face them.

Meanwhile in the living room, Jackie answered her mother's questioning look with, "Bearer bonds."

Kelly began an interrupted sentence with a W.

"They're basically as good as cash. There has to be millions of dollars worth. Do you know what this means?" Jackie said.

"Yeah," Kelly answered. "He's rich!"

"No, not that…"

"What then?" Kelly wiped her toes with the towel, again searching for the missed drops of alcohol that were causing her toes to feel sticky.

"Well," Jackie began. Then she stopped, distracted by the fact that her mother had withdrawn another stainless steel case from the briefcase and was examining its lock to see if she could open it as well. The shower had gone quiet. She took the case from her mother and placed it back into the briefcase. She closed the lid.

"What?" Kelly asked again.

"Well, I don't actually know, but it doesn't seem good. We need to put this away. We should not have seen this." Jackie just knew that Jeffrey was going to come walking out at any moment. She was scared and angry and tired all at the same time.

"It's 2-3-6, dear," Gloria said, and then when Jackie seemed to be about to ignore her, she reached out and tried to set the dials on the combination locks. Jackie spun the dials back to the positions her mother was indicating, and then just as they heard the bath door open, she handed the briefcase across the table to Kelly who put it back into its position near the leg of the coffee table. At the last second, Jackie decided she had enough time to move to her position on the sofa, but as she went, she stubbed her toe on the bowl.

Jackie was standing in front of the television, her toe smarting, and the bowl in her hand when Jeffrey entered the room. She could feel his presence and smell his scent, so she knew he was there even before she turned around. She closed her eyes and breathed softly inward through flared nostrils. "I can't thank you ladies enough for your hospitality," Jeffrey began, "I had almost forgotten there were good people in the world."

Gloria was not flustered. She never was. "That's our Jackie," she said. "She's the regular good Samaritan, especially lately."

Jackie had turned around, still holding the bowl, and was feeling dizzy. As Jeffrey was thanking her and asking if something had precipitated her move to invite him home, her eyes went dark, and she fell. The bowl landed on the coffee table spilling Kelly's replacement drink on the mail and Kelly's toes but otherwise unscathed. Meanwhile, Jackie bounced off the couch and slumped to the floor.

———≈≈≈———

"Are you okay? Can you hear me?" Jeffrey was sitting on the edge of the couch and dabbing at her forehead with a tepid rag. She raised her hand to push the rag away, and he called over his shoulder, "She's awake."

Jeffrey moved away. Gloria and Kelly swept into the opening and showered her with questions about her health and how she was feeling. She felt fine and told them so. Still, she was tired, and she should be getting to bed—this last to cover her embarrassment at swooning in front of Jeffrey. Bearer bonds and fine pectorals did not enter into her thoughts as she trudged toward her room, her own footsteps loud in her ears.

———≈≈≈———

Some time had passed since Jackie had gone to bed. Gloria and Kelly had each gone to check on her once, reporting her "sound asleepness." Jeffrey sat on the couch in Jackie's spot, the bowl on the coffee table right in front of him. He had moved his briefcase to stand near his feet.

At a lull in the conversation, Jeffrey noticed the bowl. Kelly, who was on her third cup of coffee, laced with gin and talking quickly answered, "Just some bowl."

"Actually," Gloria began. "I found that earlier today. I was thinking of having it appraised."

"What are these markings here? It appears quite old indeed." Jeffrey, who had learned a thing or two about getting your hand smacked when he had accompanied his father to art galleries as a child, was clearly restraining himself. He peered at the bowl from every reasonable angle without getting up.

"Markings?" Gloria asked, "I suppose when Jackie dropped it…"

"No, no," Jeffrey said, now turning the bowl with two fingers so that he might see the marks on the inner surface of the bowl. "They look quite intentional but somewhat incomplete."

"I honestly did not see that before," Gloria said as she moved to sit next to Jeffrey. "Do you have an interest in ancient bowls?"

"My father was an art collector," Jeffrey answered. "I suppose he was the reason I minored in archeological studies. I miss him, and it was sort of a way to bring him back. Not that—old things are cool."

As all three watched, paying more attention to the bowl than each other, a tiny white light, like burning phosphorous, lit up at the incomplete end of the markings inside the bowl. It burnt just a little way as if following a prepared track. More of a maze pattern developed on the bowl, working its way toward the center.

"What was that?" Kelly asked, leaning in. Looking at her, Jeffrey could see down her nightshirt entirely. He didn't let on but looked back toward the bowl.

"Tell me more about this bowl," Jeffrey said, still resisting the urge to pick it up and the urge to look down Kelly's neckline.

"I found it downstairs," Gloria answered. "I met my son there earlier."

"You met with Charlie?" Kelly sat up straight relieving Jeffrey and focused her attention on Gloria.

"Yes." Gloria crossed her arms at her belly and looked away.

"You didn't say anything." A tone of anger slipped into Kelly's voice.

Jeffrey was the only one who saw the etching grow toward the center and expand this time, but both women saw the light. "It did it again," he said.

"How did it go?" Kelly asked.

"Same," Gloria answered. Then a question, "What is going on with that thing?"

"I don't know," Jeffrey answered. "But it's cool. It seems to be responding to our conversation. May I touch it?"

"Oh sure," Gloria said. "If it didn't appraise well, I was thinking of using it as an ashtray."

As Jeffrey reached for the bowl, it lit, and the etching grew again. He pulled his hand quickly back. There was a faint hissing sound, and Jeffrey thought he heard a word. He stared at it intently, feeling strongly compelled to explore it.

The hall clock chimed just then, indicating two o'clock. The second chime almost shook Jeffrey to the point of wanting to write off the whole mess and get some sleep. It had been a long day, and little boys do not sleep in just because their daddy stayed up too late. No sooner had the thought formed in his mind, shaped into words, and routed to his mouth, than Kelly blurted out a bone-jarring confession.

—⁓—

The burlap wrap concealed the details of the object, but even through the rough, dense material, Charlie could feel the shape of a thick book. Twenty inches tall and a foot wide, it must have been six inches thick. The burlap fit loosely under the four leather straps.

Charlie knelt in the filth of the stall floor. Horse urine was soaking through the knees of his ruined suit pants. He did not care. By lantern light, he turned the forty-pound burlap-wrapped book over in his hands.

He was surprised and somewhat pleased to find that the straps were riveted into one another. The effect was such that with some effort, he could work the burlap out from underneath the straps. However, without cutting the leather or breaking the rivets, the intersecting straps, two in each direction, made it impossible to open the book.

He worked the burlap cover out from underneath the straps. After some effort, he could see the book almost entirely but with the straps still in place.

The binding was made of black leather, and the book had a picture of a lantern on the front. Charlie noticed the etching was of a lantern similar to the one he had with him. Under the lantern, on the corner of the book, it appeared as if a couple of words had been burned into the leather.

He shifted positions, balancing on one knee, the book perched on the other. He raised the lantern, trying to use the lantern light to examine the book's unclear markings. Under close examination, by the light of the lantern, the writing did not appear faded at all. Now he could see that the words were embossed in silver. The writing was deep set in the well-worked leather cover. It was written in English but so stylized as to be challenging to read. Alone in the muck, in the silence, in the light of the single lantern, his heart racing, he balanced precariously on one weary knee and read what appeared to be the title.

A Light.

The byline was even more startling and satisfying.

4

Late Night Confessions

"We looked in your briefcase," Kelly said. Gloria glared at her. Jeffrey looked in wonder at her smug posture. The bowl lit brightly, and a satisfyingly large section of the pattern fused into being.

Ordinarily, Jeffrey would have been angry, but all he could think about was this intriguing artifact. He managed to say, "how?" as he lifted the briefcase onto his lap and worked the combination. He flipped the lid. Everything seemed in order.

"It was Jackie's idea," Kelly lied, hoping she could ease her mother's ire. Gloria just rolled her eyes and looked away. Jeffrey left the briefcase lying on his lap, closed but unlocked. He fixed his gaze on the bowl. The pattern was nearly half-present now, and there seemed to be the tip of a tail and a bit of a wing in the maze. He wondered what else would be found. "Tell me…" he started.

"Tell us!" Kelly interrupted, sitting abruptly forward. "You're rich. Who are you? How?"

Interrupted but unshaken, Jeffrey paused then answered not knowing how this exercise would help. "I am Jeffrey Shaw. I am an architect and a bit of an art connoisseur. My stepfather was Charles Manutt. He was the only father I ever knew. Anyway, he and my mother died in a car accident when I was eleven. They were wealthy, and my dad was an art collector and trader—very successful at it. They left me a trust to be cared for by a family servant. I graduated second in my class, magna cum laude at UCLA. I finished my masters at Old Miss. I have designed and seen built over twenty structures in Mississippi, Louisiana, and Atlanta, Georgia. I'm divorced, and my ex-wife is nowhere in the picture. We came here to get a new start. I sold everything." He paused, feeling strangely compelled to be completely honest. He was telling more details from his life than he had intended and more than he usually shared. During his speaking, the bowl did not light.

"Wow," Kelly said.

"Well, we're very glad to have you in our home," Gloria said over her shoulder. She had gotten up and was standing at the drink bar pouring herself another glass of gin. She noticed the drink that she poured for Jackie earlier was still sitting on the tray, untouched. She looked toward her bedroom briefly, dropped an ice cube in the drink, and carried it back for Kelly.

When she sat back in the chair, her robe was untied and hanging open. Her red silk negligee was exposed. She sat in such a way, feet up, so that her inner thigh was exposed almost all the way up. If she had anything to say about it, Jackie would have to find her own millionaire. Her body was fit. Her mind was sharp, and her experience, she felt confident, would win the day.

There was very little pause, really. Only enough time passed for Jeffrey to will up his courage.

"After my wife left me, I lost just about everything. I was depressed. I quit working, and I started gambling heavily. Soon enough, all I had worked for was gone." Jeffrey's theory proved true, and the bowl lit. A little more of the pattern appeared as he spoke. "When I was down and out and all I had left was my son, my dad came through again."

Gloria and Kelly leaned in listening intently. They were as much watching the bowl as they were watching him. They were intrigued by his story, but then they couldn't help but be drawn to how the bowl was reacting to his story.

He continued, "I received a package in the mail. Inside was a silver cross on a chain. The cross and chain were small and elegant. There was a letter of authentication. The cross had been the cross of a martyr of the Christian faith— thousands of years old and authenticated. I really hated to do it, but I sold it at an auction. It was the last thing I had to remind me of my father. He had wanted me to have it. I accepted a very generous offer."

When he was through rattling off his confession, the room was silent except for the hissing of the bowl. The women did not seem the least bit impacted by his story. They were focused on the bowl, and only after the noise subsided and the light dimmed did they see the anguish on his face.

Gloria searched within herself for why he appeared so upset. She connected it with grief over the loss of his father. She had felt a great deal of grief over the loss of her husband even though she had never really loved him.

Still, she thought, *a good deal is a good deal.* She decided to strike deeper into her drink and to wait for him to regain his composure.

Kelly was moved almost to tears herself without really knowing why. She searched within herself and reasoned that he was a man more in touch with his emotions than any she had ever known. She decided she wanted him more than ever. As for why he was upset, she could certainly understand the loss of something so dear. Of course, he had no choice, and that too was hard for anyone to swallow. Sentimentality was not something she was into, but losing something important to you could really hurt. She knew that firsthand.

"After I sold the cross and chain, I went into an investment with a friend. It paid big. Should have been big enough to buy the cross back, but the buyer would not hear of it. Anyway, it's over now." He wiped his eyes and motioned to the bowl smugly.

5

The Asking Price

Though Jeffrey's confession about the cross had taken the pattern almost to completion, further efforts did not have much effect. For another hour, no one realized it was getting toward dawn as they told wicked tales about themselves. They confessed lured behavior of almost all types with little or no effect. Kelly even invented a few plausible tales of things she had supposedly done in college.

As the clock struck the third of five gongs in the hall, Jeffrey asked Gloria where the bowl had come from. Gloria explained in detail adding her desperate desire to sell the mansion and move on with her life. The deed doesn't have Charlie's name on it, she added, but it was his father's dying wish. Her mind was not clear, but it was more from fatigue than from alcohol. Also, there's something that she couldn't explain. She had been so distracted by the bowl that she had forgotten to finish her third drink over the intervening three hours.

The bowl sparked and fizzled a little at her telling. It was the first progress they had seen in almost an hour. Jeffrey sat up from where he had been slouched back on the couch.

"What's your asking price?" he asked. For no logical reason, he was considering doing something rash. He knew before she answered that he could afford it. He also knew he wanted it. He had driven by the mansion several times during his travels that day. It looked out of place. It was much coveted by developers having consumed prime real estate in downtown almost since its construction two hundred years before. He remembered thinking to himself that if he owned it, he would never give it up.

Gloria got up from her chair. Her legs were stiff, and she tried not to let it show, conscious of Jeffrey's eyes on her. She retrieved the prepared paperwork and handed it to him "Three million. I know I can get it, but I've been trying to...protect Charlie."

"What if," he began, "we let Charlie stay on?"

Gloria's jaw dropped slightly.

"I want it," he said. "I won't want to knock it down or resell it. I'll sign agreeing not to. I want to live there. Charlie can live there too. We can fix the place up. Run it as a bed and breakfast or something. What do you say?"

"We'd have to talk to Charlie, but it sounds good." Gloria looked toward her cell phone. She was wondering whether Charlie would answer.

6

No One Saw, No One Knew

Charlie crawled up from the stall where he had discovered the tome written or at least compiled by his father. Black had wandered off to another part of the stables, but Charlie wasn't concerned. Not only did he know that the horse could not get out but on top of that, he was more concerned about what he'd been reading in the book. The straps had proved to be no trouble after all. The rivets had popped free with surprisingly little pressure, and the inside of the book had proven even more intriguing than the surface.

For what seemed like hours, he had been hunched down in the stall pouring over page after page of the heavy gold inlaid writing. His mind raced, his heart pounded, but at last, he decided to transfer his studies to his office.

He absentmindedly left his jacket, left the door to the stables open, and left Black free to roam. He blew out the lantern only subconsciously noting how fuel efficient it had been.

He reexamined in his mind the pages he had seen as he walked. The concepts didn't make much sense to him, details of an alternate reality or an alteration of this one that could not be real, but the book had been written as if it were. The text had been completely handwritten, even copied in excerpts from other works with intricate details either voicing authenticity or proving insanity of the author. Maybe it was actually authors since much of the handwriting was different.

There was also written there, in interposing releases, details about a secret society. The secret society seemed to be an order of holy knights, and Jeffrey somehow knew his father had been one before he found the written evidence. According to the book, it was the sacred task of this order of holy knights to stop a demonic cult from completing some ritual or other and apparently had been for many centuries, possibly millennia. The concept had a ring of fiction to it. The connections in the book were hard to fathom, and even Jeffrey, who had always known his father had kept a secret, struggled with the implications of this one. He had really hoped it would be something important and somehow something more...real.

Through the mudroom off the kitchen, through the spacious kitchen, snatching an apple out of the wooden bowl on the counter, and up the winding stair in the foyer, he walked. He pushed open the office door with his butt. He turned the light switch on with his elbow and entered his father's, now his, office with comfort and familiarity.

The house was deathly quiet as it always was after eight pm when Jackson the chauffer retired to the guesthouse.

The only noise in the office came from the fish tank bubbles and the ancient wall clock. He strolled behind the desk, rolled the high-backed, black leather desk chair from its place, and laid the book on the desk's middle. He left the book closed but gently, lovingly ran his hand across its cover with his eyes closed.

It was then that the stench hit him. Covered in excrement and sweaty from his labors, he turned his own stomach. Luckily, the closet in the office held a change of clothes for him as it had for his father all the years of Jeffrey's youth. The room also had an attached shower. Showers and bathrooms were located throughout the house at convenient places; additions after much of the house's life had already passed.

In less than ten minutes, Jeffrey stood before the desk again. His mind felt more alert, and he no longer reeked. He wore jeans and a long sleeve dress shirt untucked. He had even donned a pair of tennis shoes. He wasn't sure why, but it only took a few seconds, and it seemed like the thing to do.

Thus clad, he stood back at the desk and carefully, with both hands, hoisted the book back open to the approximate place of his last reading. His heart raced as before, but what he now saw made his mouth sag open.

In the stables, quiet and dark, a faint light glowed. Charlie's jacket lay across a small crudely constructed wooden table. In its inside pocket, Charlie's cell phone glowed as an incoming call made it light up.

Black stood over the table. He turned his head sideways so he could look the little light square in his eye. He nudged the jacket so that it fell open.

The phone's screen read, "1 missed call: Mother." Black looked at the screen and then looked at the mansion through the open stables door. High in the mansion, he could see bright light in one window.

As the light on the phone went out, a feint, reddish hue lit and ebbed slightly brighter in the horse's eyes. It died quickly, softly, and without consequence as it had begun. With it died the last remnants of a long-stored hope, but no one knew because no one saw.

Black wandered back to his stall. He passed the now-darkened lantern Charlie had been using to study the book. He swung around in his cell, edged out far enough to unlatch the rope, and pulled the door shut with his chin. The wringing clank of the latching cell door unheard, he stood there in his stall and dozed off. The last feint remembrance of a different time had been washed away by old age and the pain in his joints.

The pages of the book were now blank! He flipped hurriedly through every page, even those he had not seen yet getting angry with himself. He picked the book up, closed it again, and reopened it again. Nothing!

No use! The writing was gone. The gold-embossed trim was gone. Not one drop of ink remained! What trickery was this? He should have known it had all been too easy!

He slammed the book shut; a small cloud of dust scattered out onto his desk calendar. He flopped down in the chair and spun away from the desk. He lowered his head into his hands and then tried hard to think what was different. A feeling of despair settled over him.

Nothing was right. He had screwed up. He had come to the office for his own comfort, and now he had somehow lost what he had been searching for. The outcome of years of labor had been lost in an instant! He had been so close to all he had been searching for, so close to answers and now, nothing! Tears welled up in his eyes, and his stomach churned. All he could think about was how badly he had messed up.

After a moment, he fell to his knees on the floor. He put his hands over his head as if protecting himself from falling debris. He felt as if he were getting smaller and smaller.

———

Three million dollars in transferred bearer bonds plus room and board for Charlie for life as long as he desired to stay in exchange for the mansion and the bowl. That was the agreement.

The deal was struck; the paperwork was signed, the bowl all but forgotten during the negotiations. Kelly returned from her room with her notary seal and prepared to stamp the document. Jeffrey's driver's license lay on the coffee table. Lost earlier, it had conveniently turned up inside the briefcase. Drunk with fatigue and excited over the prospects of doing business in such a reckless yet apparently efficient way, no one thought much of that or of any of the other strange coincidences. Gloria returned from checking on the children.

Jeffrey began to tidy up. He placed the driver's license, the pen he had been signing over the bonds with, and the bowl in the briefcase. Gloria almost said something when the bowl went out of sight, but just at that moment, Kelly spoke.

"Here goes," she said. She really meant nothing by it, just that an era of their lives was ending. She only meant that after that stamp was applied, there was no going back, and none of the three of them had any idea just how right she was. She squeezed the seal hard, and the deal was official.

Gloria sat in her chair. She held the three million in bearer bonds in a stack on her lap, her forearms crossed over them. "It's over," she said, softly.

"It'll be dawn soon," Jeffrey said.

"It feels like dawn now," Kelly said, sliding the seal back into its pouch.

With that, they retired. The women had forgotten their physical attraction to Jeffrey. Jeffrey lowered himself back onto the couch. He found himself wondering why, if he had just done something right, really right, for the first time in his life, why was he feeling so guilty? Why did he feel such a sense of impending doom?

Gloria pulled the vertical blind shut in her east-facing bedroom, blocking out every fragment of the predawn light possible. She adjusted the comfort level of her bed. She slid into her silk sheets, the chill an extra comfort somehow.

She ordered her voice-activated alarm to wake her at 9 AM. The face of the clock read 6:45 AM, and she sighed knowing she would be very tired. Still, she wanted to get to the bank not long after they opened. She fell asleep clutching the stack of bearer bonds. She was very pleased with herself but somehow sadder than she expected.

Kelly put her things away and flopped down on her bed. She pressed the power button on the TV remote and expected it to turn on. She never really looked at it, drifting off to sleep in seconds. The picture on the TV was frozen. A black-suit clad announcer sat at a desk with a picture of a ship in a little square behind him. His mouth stood open as if he was speaking, but he sat motionless and silent. Kelly did not notice as she quickly fell asleep and slept restlessly.

Jackie slept peacefully. She did not know of the betrayal of her mother. She slept oblivious to the deal, ignoring her father's dying wish. The mansion had been sold. She knew nothing of the further revealed properties of the bowl.

Next to the couch in the briefcase, nestled next to the remaining bearer bonds, other important papers, and Jeffrey's handgun, the bowl began to glow. For one instant, in the darkened living room, it glowed so brightly that one could see it right through the metal shell of the briefcase. But again, no one saw, no one knew.

The Moment Begins

Jeffrey leapt to his feet, his head spun a little due to the quick rise from the couch. The women rushed into the living room, and all four met at the door to the kids' room. A loud crash had woken them all, and the smell of acrid smoke filled the apartment and stoked their worry.

Jeffrey turned the knob and threw open the door. A wisp of smoke swept into the living room. He slung the door open so hard that the door handle stuck in the drywall.

Without hesitation, all four filed into the room. Kelly stopped just inside the door with her hand over her mouth. Jeffrey picked up the empty bedding and checked the bed. Gloria walked dazed out into the center of the room and stared in amazement at the hole in the wall.

The windows were gone completely. A portion of the wall to either side was missing as well, leaving a hole big enough to drive a truck through. The drapes clung to the rods and whipped violently in the night air. Stories below the streetlights lit a foggy night with an eerie yellow gloom. In the far distance, the predawn light reflected off clouds like a field of cotton candy growing up from the horizon and spreading in all directions.

"What's this?" Gloria asked Jeffrey who was storming around in a circle through the room lost in blinding fury before his eyes stopped to look.

The four of them quickly formed a semicircle around a spiral staircase that led down into the floor of the room. Smoke slowly rolled up the stairs and added to the smoky haze at their feet. The bitterness of the smoke made their throats ache and their eyes water.

"Where did this come from?" Jeffrey demanded and then directly to Jackie. "This wasn't here before! Was it?"

Jackie mutely shook her head no. Kelly slid down against the wall as far as the floor and began to sob. Jeffrey dashed back into the living room and returned quicker than the women could follow. He had snatched up his case and went directly to the stairs.

"What are you doing?" Jackie cried.

"I'm calling the police," Gloria said, disappearing into the living room.

"Where's my son? Where's Buddy?" Jeffrey shouted into Jackie's face.

"I don't know!" she yelled.

Jeffrey began to descend the spiral staircase, taking two steps at a time. Jackie looked at Kelly who was in a daze, looked toward the living room, and then followed Jeffrey down the stairs.

—◦◦◦—

Charlie lifted his head. How long had he been lying there? His tears were dried, but his face still felt a bit tacky. He rose to his feet. Had he passed out? The wall clock said it had only been a short time. He looked at the book on the desk.

He opened the book gently, hoping to see writing. Nothing. He shut the book again. This time he was not sad. He thought, *Tomorrow is another day.*

A noise in the hall caught his attention. He looked at the clock. Could it be that Sally, the maid, came to work early? However, this time a shadow covered the wall clock so he could not make out the time. The picture window framed predawn light, and the light pierced the room, but still he could not see the clock face. A noise in the hall caught his attention again, close, slightly louder.

He snatched up the book and stuffed it in the bottom file drawer on the desk. He crept toward the door. He heard the shrill squeal of a fire alarm going off somewhere far off in the house.

As he crept toward the door, he hefted a fire poker from near the fireplace. Tense, dramatic, horror movie music began to play in the recesses of his mind. He thought to himself how he and his sister had yelled at the characters moving slowly toward the suspicious noise. *No, don't go in there, you idiot!* He stalked toward the door anyway, raising the poker in a traditional two-handed batter's grip.

The squeaky floorboard outside the door that he knew all to well squeaked. Often his father had known he was there before even he knocked, and it wasn't until Charlie was ten or so that he had figured out how. Charlie slowly reached for the door handle.

He began to turn it ever so gently. The music was louder now, but curiosity had him in its grasp.

Just as the lock cleared the catch, the door flew open. Charlie caught a glimpse of a man in a white tuxedo with a satin lapel and a blood red flower in his breast pocket. In a flash though, the man grew, his face stretched, became grotesque, like that of a beast. He filled the doorway completely.

Charlie swung the poker overhead full force. But the beast, whose white suit disappeared in a flash, easily fended off the blow with one grotesque forearm. It ducked under the doorframe and stepped in toward Charlie. Charlie tried to scream. His voice cracked, and nothing came out.

The beast raised a mighty clawed arm and swung a wide ark. Charlie could easily have dodged, but he stood frozen in fear. The talons of the beast's hands ripped into him. The beast fell on him and finished him off.

The spiral staircase emptied out into an alcove of a much larger room. The room was a throne room of sorts. In fact, it was the one that Gloria and Charlie had visited earlier that day. Wispy gray smoke filled the edges and spread toward the center of the room growing shallower until only random tendrils drifted across from side to side. The smoke covered the alcove too, and so the room's occupants were somewhat surprised when Jeffrey and Jackie dashed into their midst.

In the center of the room, clear of the smoke, stood two tables made of heavy wood and crude construction. Manacles dangled at the head and foot of each. Across the large room from the alcove, a man and a woman sat upon two thrones. This couple wore dark skin and colorful African-style gowns. The man now rose to his feet and at the same time, a dozen or so men closed in from the edges of the room covered by the smoke only to their knees now.

Two of the crowd of men were of particular interest. They stood nearest to the man and woman armed with shield and spear, and they looked like extras from a Zulu movie. Jackie and Jeffrey had seen the old Zulu movies and knew the weapons could be deadly. What's more, snarling looks of intensity reaching out from behind their face paint screamed bloodthirstiness.

"Welcome," said the man.

Jeffrey edged forward to be directly opposite to the man across the tables. His mind was reeling at the thought of what the tables looked as if they might be suited for. He fidgeted at the combination of the briefcase, and in a second, it was unlocked.

"Why have you come?" The man's voice had the rhythmic undertones of a cello and boomed throughout the hall.

"We are looking for two small children," Jackie answered as she saw the desperate look on Jeffrey's face. She wondered why he didn't answer.

"We have the children." There was an edge of suspicion in the man's voice. "Has there been news of the object?"

Jackie noticed him look knowingly toward the men to their right. She realized the men were closing the intervening distance during the conversation. She looked at Jeffrey. He was watching the front of the room staring down the king. (That's what she thought the guy was.)

"No!" Jackie yelled, raising her hands, palms outward and circling around Jeffrey. "Back off! Leave us alone! We don't want any trouble!"

"We just want…" Jeffrey started.

The king shouted at the men who were seemingly held off by Jackie. "Bring them to me!"

"We cannot, my lord," One of the men answered in cockney English that somehow contrasted his pinstriped suit.

"Really?" the king asked incredulously. "No, really?"

There was a pause during which Jeffrey finished his sentence. "The children," he said.

Then he turned to Jackie, "What's going on?"

"I'm not sure," she answered.

The king turned back to his throne. He plopped down, straightening his robes. Then with a heavy disgusted sigh, he said, "Get them."

Two men with spears and shields somehow knew he was talking to them and after looking at one another, began to edge forward. They leveled their spears and picked up speed as they came. Their eyes narrowed, and they focused on Jeffrey.

Jackie rotated around Jeffrey and with her hands raised, shouted, "Stop!" She was hoping for another miracle. The other men had listened. Why not these two? But it didn't work.

The men were at a full run now and had already covered half of the thirty-foot distance. There was no time to dodge. There was no time for anything. Jackie cringed under the imminent impact of the razor-edged spears. There really was nothing else she could do.

8

Upstairs and
in through the Window

Charlie awoke with a start and jumped off the floor. His nightmare had been all too realistic. He immediately looked at the clock. He wiped the remainder of his tears from his face and looked out the window. The scene out the window was precisely the same as it had been in his dream.

His heart racing, he stood behind the desk and opened the book. Still blank. He shut the book and picked it up.

A noise in the hall sent a chill down his spine and he froze. His mind was struggling to sort dream from reality. Then it occurred to him that it didn't matter. There shouldn't be any noises in the house at sunrise.

Shaken from his daze, he leapt into action. He rushed across the room to the fireplace. The squeaky board outside the door squeaked telling of someone's presence.

Charlie looked over his shoulder curious about what or who lay beyond the door. He pressed a whitewashed stone in the fireplace, and as it slid, a section equal to about half of the fireplace also slid back out of the way. He slipped into the secret passage and closed the secret door behind him.

———✦✦✦———

Two shots, like miniature explosions rang through the throne room. Both spearmen were carried off their feet as the rounds impacted one in the head and the other in the chest.

One spear grazed Jackie's cheek. A thin line of blood appeared. Two of the men from the smoke edged forward, but then seeing Jackie still standing, they stopped.

Jackie's eyes widened as she turned to see Jeffrey now pointing a .357 revolver at the king. As she was facing off the spearmen, Jeffrey had obviously retrieved the pistol from his case. The preciseness of the kill shots testified to long hours of training with the weapon.

"Now, listen to me!" Jeffrey yelled. "We want the kids! Now! The next one I shoot is you!"

Fear flashed across the king's face. "They are not here. They were taken to the mansion."

"What mansion?" Jeffrey asked. "Kerromyer mansion?" Jeffrey cast Jackie a knowing glance. "What is going on?"

"Yes," the king replied. "They are to be prepared."

"For what?" Jeffrey asked.

The king just spread his arms to indicate the tables before him. They were to be prepared for sacrifice.

———✦✦✦———

Gloria was explaining to Kelly that the phones were not working when Jackie and Jeffrey erupted from the staircase back into the nursery. The curtains hung limply half inside and half outside the wounded building, and the sunrise remained frozen in place.

Jeffrey pushed the wardrobe over until it fell partly into the spiral staircase. "Does anyone know what is going on? Gloria!"

Gloria shook her head, no.

"I've got to know where my son is!" He waved the pistol around to emphasize the point.

"Jeffrey, you killed those men," Jackie said.

"What?" Kelly spoke for the first time since she had collapsed against the wall, and her "What" drowned out Jeffrey's, "So what?"

"There were a bunch of men down there. They attacked me, and he shot two." She stabbed her finger at Jeffrey.

"I need answers! You ain't seen nothin' yet!" Jeffrey yelled.

"I think I can help with that," a voice spoke from the opening overlooking the street.

Charlie pushed through the curtains on a horse.

A large black stallion with flaming hooves entered the room from the predawn sky. On its back rode Charlie. Jeffrey pointed the .357 at him.

"Charlie?" Gloria asked as he swung down from the saddle.

"I got here as quick as I could," Charlie said, stifling a smile.

Necessary Preparations

"The nearest I can figure we've entered into something called the the Moment," Charlie explained. "According to the book I found, Dad was a member of a group called the Paladins, and their whole purpose was to enter the Moment and thwart the plans of an evil cult."

"We've met them," Jackie inserted. "Downstairs."

"Then they must be huge because there's a bunch of them at the house too," Charlie said. "Anyway, somehow the Paladins could stop them. Don't you see? I'm gonna have to do that now!"

"They have my son," Jeffrey snapped.

"And Jacob," Jackie added.

"Yikes!" Charlie was talking as fast as he could, but everyone was very excited, and he couldn't keep up. "We'd better act fast. I read these guys are into child sacrifice."

"They took them to the mansion." Jeffrey was strapping on his shoulder holster and stuffing speed loaders into his pockets.

While the three of them were sorting out what was going, on Black edged up to Gloria. She met him halfway. They lay their heads against each other, forehead to forehead, and she stroked his neck.

"I've missed you." She was thinking and maybe said it out loud softly. She thought she heard a soft voice in her head say, "I missed you too." Just then, she was shaken by Jackie.

"Mom, are you okay?" Jackie asked.

"Yeah, sure. I mean as much as can be expected." Gloria craned her head and looked at Black's still smoking hooves. The old horse had regained his youthful vigor. The sagging, which had crept in over the years, was all but gone. Rock firm muscles like those from his horse racing days had returned.

"He's the Paladin's warhorse," Charlie said. "His actual name is Coal. He's in the book." He moved to join her near Coal, the horse formerly known as Black.

"Did the book tell you he was the Paladin's warhorse?" Gloria asked a hint of doubt in her voice as she stroked the mane of the big black stallion.

"No, actually I made that part up. It talks about when Dad bought him, and that he had been involved with the Moment from before then, but that's really all. I mostly just read the first part of the book, which is about how Dad got involved with the Paladins and his history and such..." His voice trailed off.

"Where's the book now?" Jackie asked. As she asked, she placed a firm hand on Charlie's shoulder and turned him back toward herself and Jeffrey.

"I..." Charlie started to answer.

"Who cares!" Jeffrey broke in. "We've got to save those kids. This is my son we're talking about here!"

"And mine too," Kelly added. Everyone turned to see that she was just stepping into the doorway of the room with a baseball bat in her hands and dressed to travel.

It was just then that the others realized how they were dressed. They looked down at themselves and then at each other. In unison, they headed for the door while Charlie stood, nodding in agreement.

"Be right with you," Jeffrey said politely as he passed Kelly. Jackie and Gloria passed her in a gust. They threw off night clothes as they reached their rooms and quickly dressed in things more appropriate.

10

Passed Away but Not Forgotten

In her closet, Jackie found some work-out gear—sports bra and Under Armour. She put it on, and then sliding aside her regular wardrobe, she chose some clothes from her past: leather pants, a leather jacket, and her soft leather boots. She decided to forego the spiked heels, figuring they would just slow her down.

At the dresser, Jackie pinned and bound back her hair. She slipped a simple belt through the loops on her leather pants. Sliding open the sock drawer, she shoved the socks aside, and her stiletto slid into view. As she reached for it, she had a thought.

She remembered Pastor Dan counseling her to get rid of the trappings of her old life. He had said that in an instant, she could lose control. In an instant, she could be trapped by who she once was. She looked in the mirror.

Dressed in leather, the stiletto in her hand, she saw yesterday far too clearly. She pressed the button, and the blade of the stiletto leapt out. *This is important*, she thought. She stood frozen, watching in the mirror as video clips of her life played in her mind.

There was a roadhouse bar, and the guy she'd been sharing drinks and conversation with was down on the floor, his face bloodied. Standing over him was the six-foot-two, hairy, rotund reason for his pain. She dropped to one knee next to her fallen friend.

The big guy reached down with both hands to grab his prey, and he came back up with a bloody nose as Jackie elbowed him in the face. She could see her drinking acquaintance was in no shape to get up and defend himself. Though she didn't know his name, she rose to her feet and interposed herself between him and his assailant.

No telling whether big burly man would normally have hit a girl. He touched his tongue to the flow of blood on his upper lip, narrowed his eyes, and took a swing.

Jackie easily ducked under the meaty fist and arm. The half-squat hiked her miniskirt, increasing her mobility. She sprang up quickly and shoved the off-balance attacker so that he reeled forward and slammed his face into the bar. She grabbed her downed friend by the ankle and slid him clear as burly man fell in his place.

—◦◦◦—

Another scene, this time on a dark street. A nearby street light flickered on and off, buzzing constantly.

Jackie was with two friends from work. They'd been clubbing and were dressed skimpy. They were chilled by the night air. Steam was still rising as they cooled from sweaty activity in the night club. Nearing the car, they were intercepted. Three pretty girls meet two men on a dark street at night. The men covered their faces with ski masks.

"Purses, ladies, and put your hands on the car," said the front guy. He waved a stiletto to accent his words.

Jackie and her friends moved to follow the instructions, but Jackie made sure she was the closest to the muggers. The muggers came behind and took the purses, and if they were just muggers, they should have ran. But they didn't, and Jackie had feared they wouldn't.

Wendy, who was next to Jackie, drew in a deep breath as the mugger came near to take her purse. That was the bait.

The masked mugger grabbed Wendy's ponytail, pulled her head back, and raised the knife.

Jackie leapt into action. She grabbed the mugger's knife hand and opposite shoulder, twisting the arm behind his back. Her knee against the back of his, she spun him over and toward the ground. Momentum and gravity slammed the side of his head into the pavement.

The second man moved in. Without looking, Jackie shot her left foot out, firmly planting her spiked heal in the rapidly approaching groin. The man crumpled immediately, but momentum carried him head first into the pavement next to his friend.

"Start the car!" Jackie hissed at the girls as she sprung to her feet and picked up the stiletto and the purses. She looked at the stiletto.

She liked it. It was like her then. It was quick, sharp, and wicked.

Later, she would tell her friends that she had been taking a self-defense class, but that was a lie of course. She had learned every last move on the street, in the school of hard knocks. Her parents had money, but Jackie wasn't into the pampered, sheltered life her sister had chosen. They had money, but they had longtime lost control of Jackie. She could do as she pleased as long as she learned to take care of herself and so she did. She had more than a few physical scars to show for it, even more emotional ones.

———

There she was again. She was standing outside the New Heights church mission. It was the night she got stopped for her DUI, then in church, then at the dining room table in her run-down flat with Pastor Dan and his wife until all hours of the night.

Then she saw herself at the altar giving her life to God. There she was, coming out of the baptismal waters, and she had kept her eyes open because she wanted to see.

Then back in the present, as she thought about how much she loved Jesus, she let the stiletto roll off her hand and back into the sock drawer. She pushed the drawer shut with her thighs and smiled meekly in the mirror.

"Good girl," she said. As she left the room, she grabbed a pair of low, soft boots for Kelly.

"Lose the heels," she said, handing Kelly the boots as she reentered the nursery. Kelly wore her boots, but they had three-inch heels.

Charlie, Black, and Jeffrey were not in the room.

"Where'd they go?" Jackie asked.

"The mansion," Kelly answered with a grunt removing her boots.

"Faster than the elevators, I suppose," Jackie said, moving to look down toward the street. The scene was surreal. The sun had still not moved. The colors of the dawn were reflecting beautifully but eerily off the glass skyscrapers of downtown. Cars on the street stood frozen in place, sitting right where they had apparently been when "the Moment" began.

"Elevators don't work," Kelly answered. "Nothing does. TVs are frozen, clocks, phones, cars, everything."

"Too weird," Jackie said.

"I always knew your father was up to no good," Gloria said.

"Mom," Kelly scolded. "According to Charlie, Dad was the good guy here."

"Oh, right." Gloria drifted off into amazement as she stepped up to view through the broken wall. She could see Charlie on Coal soaring across the open sky. A trail of flames followed each hoof, and only just now, the horse seemed to be slowing to a speed where his image was not blurred by movement.

11

The View from a Nightmare

Moment. (noun) Literally an indefinite brief period of time; an instant.

Moment of Truth. (a) The moment in a bull fight when a matador faces the bull for the kill (b) A critical moment in time which tests or reveals one's true self or makes one face the truth. (c) A period of time, brief but long enough for the completion of the events in question

Flying over, the city left Kelly dumbfounded. The traffic, although scarce at dawn, was never nonexistent. In the Moment, cars, trucks, and even a motorcycle were frozen in place. She had even seen a FedEx truck frozen in mid-turn; its blinker locked in the on position. The street lights were all lit, but persons and vehicles alike were frozen in place.

In keeping with her own perceptions of her ever-present bad luck, she felt something spatter on her shoulder. She looked to see bird poop. Looking up, she realized they had just flown under a flock of gulls suspended in midair.

She shook her head in disgust. She gritted her teeth and wondered at that. Bird poops at the exact instant the Moment begins. Poop suspends in midair. Kelly flies into poop. Really? She had just about accepted the incredible possibility when she saw the mansion and lost her sanity again.

The grounds of the mansion were much larger than she remembered them being. She remembered at least twice when she had been younger when the city had confiscated portions of the estate grounds to build roads. Now, as Black carried her and Charlie near to the grounds, she surmised that she was seeing them in their former glory. Where the ruins had always been on the southeastern corner of the mansion, a grand tower now stood, forty feet in diameter and at least eighty feet tall. The pool was gone. There were several outbuildings that she didn't remember, and the gardens stretched in every direction for a mile at least.

Signs of the city's intrusion remained. In the middle of the south garden, surrounded and almost overcome by three willow trees, she could see a semitrailer. West of there in another version must have been an intersection because stop lights rose above the garden, vines clinging to them, and yellow light emanated from them. Clearly, the mansion had returned to its former glory over top of the city's new constructs.

However, in at least one case, what had been built had been erased. At the farthest eastern corner of the grounds, a skyscraper butted up to and would have extended into the garden. In the Moment, the third of the skyscraper that would have jutted out into the garden was absent. The effect was to expose the innards of the building. Office furniture on the twentieth floor jutted out into space. It looked as if filing cabinets, desks, tables, and in many cases people, were about to fall many stories to the garden below. None did however, because in the Moment, the skyscraper and its contents were suspended in time.

"Unbelievable," Kelly said, clinging even tighter to Charlie as they swooped down toward the side stables. In the new—or rather old version—it appeared on the grounds there were three sets of stables, and the track they'd grown up playing on was the smaller of two.

"Isn't it?" Charlie responded. The excitement in his voice contrasted Kelly's solemn wonder. Charlie noticed her quivering and asked if she was cold.

"No," she responded. She tightened her muscles to try to make the quivering stop. That only made it worse. She was afraid. She was more afraid now than at any time in her life. She was thinking to herself just how wrong all this was and how she really wasn't supposed to be here when the horse's hooves hit cobblestone, and Jeffrey stepped forward to help her down. She swung her leg over and fell into his arms.

He supported her weight easily and carried her to a nearby bail of hay.

12

The Book Interrupted

"Anything in the book?" Charlie asked, swinging down. His legs were a little stiff, but somehow he felt strangely energized after ferrying everyone here.

It was Gloria who had figured out the mystery of the book. She had remembered her husband sitting up for long hours doing something at his desk. She thought she remembered a pot of ink and an old-fashioned pen from one time when she'd unintentionally snuck up on him.

One thing she'd remembered for sure. Every time she'd come near, he had blown out the lamp. She had always thought it peculiar that he'd used that old lamp.

However, once when visiting her sister, she had noticed a similar lamp on her brother-in-law's desk. It didn't match the desk or the room. She had made a little quip about it, meaning nothing really at the time.

"That's Bryan's," her sister had said. "He simply will not get rid of it. He says books are best read by the light in which they are written. Bryan likes old books." The quaint smiles and a motion to Bryan's library ended the conversation. At the time, Gloria hadn't cared that much anyway.

On hearing Charlie's story about the print in the book disappearing, Gloria put the two events together immediately. They had retrieved the book from the hiding place, split the darkness with the small lamp's flame, and began pouring over the book's pages for answers while they waited for each member of the little group. Gloria and then Jackie had the most time on it.

Jeffrey kept watch for trouble; he paced from one side of the stables to the other with the revolver in his hand. The revolver was a very comfortable extension of his arm. He'd been shooting handguns since he could walk. Right now, he really wanted to take off after his son. But he felt responsible for protecting the others, and besides he didn't know where to start. Somehow, he knew that they were all in this together.

"Here's something," Gloria said. "It says it's taken from another book written by someone who survived the Moment."

"You mean this has happened before?" Charlie asked.

"Apparently," Gloria answered before continuing to read out loud the excerpt.

Taken from the Journal of Jedediah Wolfe, written about 1879, found 2003, decoded 2004, and destroyed 2005.

Jedediah, a trainer in the Moment, writes:

Today, when the sun fully rose for the first time in what seemed like a week, I began to believe it was really over. Of course it rained last night, almost all day yesterday, rain like crying, thick seemingly endless tears.

Celia is dead. I had hoped when reality returned she'd be alive again, like at the end of a bad dream, but no. We'll be burying her today, I reckon.

Harper's gut cut, and an ordinary fella wouldn't survive it, but I'm not sure for him. 'Cause he's strong like a mule and big like an ox. Still, he loved Celia before she died and that makes me wonder too.

I had lunch and drinks with Charlie Putnam. He's saying he's headed back east. He says even though he'll never ride another horse like ole Cole, he's headed for Kentuck where he can race most of the year.

He says it'll happen again. He says he and some of his kind have always known. He was worth a lot in the Moment even though he was caught off-guard. He says not in our lifetime, but it'll happen again. I reckon that's part of why I'm writing this. Maybe it'll help somehow—I mean for the next time.

For our time, here are some facts:

The head man's name is Nero. Except he isn't a man. Celia says he's an evil spirit or demon or something. It's bad, on account of he's still out there somewhere.

There was five of us. Almost from the beginning, Putnam figured out what was going on. It wasn't until well after the pattern of the bowl was finished; he remembered one or more of us was going to have to die. I was real sore at him at the time, but he proved himself, and he said it had to be, and I believed him—we all did.

One thing, it would have been good to know from the beginning was about the bowl and the sacrifice. We figured right away that completing the pattern started the Moment and that we had to 'cause in between the real world and the Moment is even worse. The sacrifice opens up Nero and his cult to kill humans like during the in-between but permanent like. Two innocent kids and that bowl, that's all he needs.

Could be in other times things were different. Seems like we had some clues; that might be the case.

The five of them had been so engrossed in reading the journal entry that they almost missed the sounds of footsteps and the opening of the stables' doors at the west entrance. Jeffrey was the first to catch it and he rushed them out into the garden.

13

Run and Hide

The garden was cool but moist. A varying level of mist hung at different places among the bushes. Amidst a huge mound of lilac bushes, an opening in the middle served for cover. They hunkered down to wait. Jeffrey lay the briefcase down and offered Jackie to sit on it.

Jackie passed the offer to Gloria who accepted. Kneeling on the ground, sitting on her ankles, Jackie opened the book on her lap to the page she marked with her finger as they ran.

Jeffrey watched as two men in plain gray suits with mirrored shades stood at the entrance to the stables where they had just been. The man on the right had a wide nose to match his wide shoulders and sniffed at the air. It was as if he knew someone was near and could track them by scent. After a short delay, he slowly raised his left arm and pointed in the general direction of the lilac mound.

Jeffrey pulled back the hammer on the revolver. He closed his eyes and let out a long breath, shaking his head gently.

Meanwhile, Gloria had scooted over on the case and offered half her seat to Kelly. Kelly declined. Gloria offered the seat to Jackie who absentmindedly got up and scooted onto the case.

Jeffrey edged out of the lilac bushes along the ground. He lay ten feet from the others. He took aim with the revolver. His mind flitted back to the silenced 9mm he had sold the previous year, silencer and all. He liked the feel of the .357 but missed the ability to be quiet. A .357 Magnum is not a quiet thing—except maybe as a club.

The men moved to separate and work their way into the garden. But just as they started to part, the sniffer lashed out with his right arm and stopped the other guy. They looked at each other in silence, their glasses reflecting each others' faces. The sniffer shook his head, and then abruptly, they turned and headed back through the stables.

When Jeffrey returned to the group, Jackie and Gloria were sitting on the case. The book was closed. Jeffrey must have had a quizzical look on his face.

"We need the lamp," she said. In fact, Charlie had carried the lamp with them to the garden; but in the bright light here, the pages of the book were blank.

"Of course," Jeffrey said. Then, realizing that she had been answering the look on his face, he continued, "That's not it. Something just happened."

"Seriously?" Kelly asked, sounding angry. She motioned to the split open skyscraper. "We're in the Moment!"

"Get a hold of yourself, Kelly," Gloria said. "What is it? What did you see?"

"Those two guys were standing at the door there. They, the one guy acted like he could smell us. He even pointed in our direction then suddenly, they turned around and left."

"Why?" Jackie asked.

"My point exactly," Jeffrey snapped back.

"Maybe they could smell the lamp," Charlie chimed in. "I put it out not long after we ran."

"Could be..." Jeffrey's voice trailed off.

"No," Gloria said. "That's not it."

"What then?" Kelly asked.

Jackie and Gloria slid off the case. They spun around as if they both had the same thought. Before they could even open the case, all could see the dull orange glow of the bowl inside.

"The bowl," Jeffrey said softly.

Gloria opened the case. The light from the bowl, which glowed brilliant orange and red hues, was seemingly brighter than the rising sun. In the far distance from the mansion, they heard a shriek as of some great beast had stubbed its toe. There was a great sound of breaking glass and something that sounded like sailcloth snapping against a strong wind.

Jeffrey spun and aimed the revolver in the direction of the house. He could see the bright starburst remaining before his eyes. Kelly's eyes had been closed in dread, and so she was not blinded but felt helpless just the same. Charlie wiped at his eyes and cringed back into the thin chokers of the lilac bushes.

Gloria groped to shut the case, somehow understanding that the light would draw trouble. But Jackie held the case open, and in a second, the light went out. Everyone's vision cleared. They cringed undercover, knowing that what was coming was coming from above and was something that they had not yet seen.

Jackie lay on top of the bowl, which issued no more light than if it were painted with glow-in-the-dark paint. The light had gone out as soon as she had grabbed it. Sharp chokers scratched at her legs, but it just felt like pressure as her leather breaches protected her.

Everyone lay undercover but peeked through the gaps in the branches, leaves, and flowers to see what was coming. A ten-foot tall humanoid form with a twenty-foot wingspan soared over head. He looked more like a massive hairless ape than a human. His long leathery wings and all his toes and fingers were tipped with black, filed-to-a-point nails. His genitals, which apparently were centrally located like that of a man, lie discretely behind a black fur loincloth. The loincloth and similarly constructed black, fur bracers adorning his wrists served as his only clothing.

Jackie could hear Kelly's voice somewhere behind her, saying softly, over and over, "Oh my god. Oh my god."

Jackie wanted to move to comfort her sister but knew she dare not lest the beast spot her. So she pressed even farther back into the chokers, clasped her hands together as a little child prays, and did the only thing she could think to do. She prayed.

She begged God to comfort Kelly. She begged him to turn back the demon. She prayed, *God, you know we need help. You know we don't know what we are doing, and you know we need time.*

As she prayed, she was unaware of just how close the beast was to passing over their exact position. With each pass over the garden, he was nearing to flying dead overhead. He swooped around the damaged skyscraper, and

Jeffrey prepared to take a shot. This last pass would bring him right down on them. Jackie opened her eyes to see this as she prayed out loud but softly, "God, turn him away and make him forget he ever saw us. Give us some time, God, to find out what is going on." As she prayed, she knew in her heart that one of two things would be true. Either God would intercede, or they would die right there in the garden, surrounded by lilacs.

She wasn't as surprised as she thought she would be. The beast pulled up abruptly. His wings beat hard to keep him hovering in midair. Twenty feet from their position and no more than forty feet above them, it was even possible he was looking right at them.

Jeffrey hesitated just long enough, and the beast was gone. He whipped around with great agility and wafted lazily back toward the main house.

A long pause before anyone would move. Then it was Kelly who broke the silence. She had crawled back into the open area in the center on all fours.

"What the heck was that?" she asked.

"Demon," Charlie answered with a matter-of-fact tone in his voice. He had crawled back to the opening in the center of the lilac bushes as well.

"I guess he didn't like these flowers," Jeffrey said.

"Lilacs," Gloria corrected."

"Who cares?" Jeffrey's tone was agitated.

"Apparently, he did," Gloria answered.

"It wasn't the flowers, er, lilacs," Jackie said, adding the last when she saw her mother's mouth come open. "It was God. God protected us."

"Oh, c'mon," Kelly began.

"I'm not kidding," Jackie said. She had read the incredulous looks on every face but one. The fact that her mother seemed to be buying her explanation surprised her since her mother had actually scolded her when she had shared her decision to follow Christ.

"Now is not the time for faith stuff," Jeffrey snapped. "We've got real problems here."

"What better time?" Jackie faced Jeffrey in particular as all five stood in the middle of the opening of the bushes.

Kelly stepped near to Jeffrey and said quietly, "Jackie became a Christian a while back, and since then, this stuff keeps coming up."

"This stuff?" Jackie was getting upset. "Mom!"

Everyone looked at Gloria. Kelly was holding onto Jeffrey's arm. Charlie had the book between his legs and the lamp and bat in his hands.

"Well," Gloria spoke softly and slowly. "It actually makes sense. Or at least it had better. Think about it. If demons are real here, why not God?"

"God is real everywhere, Mom," Jackie said.

"Right, well now we've seen a demon so maybe, but why do you think God intervened? What did you see?"

At that, Jeffrey had enough. "We have to move! I say Charlie and I go up to the house and try to save the kids while you guys hide somewhere and—" He already knew it wasn't going to fly by the looks on their faces, but as an afterthought, he tried to sweeten the deal, "and study the book?"

"No," the three women said almost simultaneously, and Charlie breathed a sigh of relief.

"I need a holy sword or something before I go charging in anywhere," Charlie said.

No one made the connection he was thinking that he was the Paladin, and there was an uncomfortable pause. "Besides, I told you in the house…dozens…not enough bullets."

"If anyone's going to the house, it's me," Jackie said. "I'm protected."

"By God?" Jeffrey asked.

"Yeah."

"I don't think so," Jeffrey said.

"Listen," Gloria commanded. "Why don't we just destroy the bowl? They need it for whatever their trying, right?"

"You think that'll work?" Jackie asked.

"It can't be that simple," Charlie said.

"You wouldn't think so," Gloria answered. "But the only thing we have to lose is if they kill the kids in anger."

"Then, no," Jeffrey said, "Too risky."

"We need more information." Gloria grabbed the book from between Charlie's legs and clenched it to her chest.

"Fine," Jeffrey said. "You guys take the book somewhere and read. Charlie and I will go try to figure out where they are holding the kids. We won't try anything until we have more information both ways unless we see it's now or never to save the kids."

While everyone else was still considering the proposal, Jackie spoke up. "Fine, but you and I go, and Charlie goes with them. I'm protected. I'm telling you."

She wasn't sure it was true. But somehow the more they seemed to refuse it, the more sure she was.

"Fine," Jeffrey said.

"I want to go," Kelly said.

"No," all four of the others said almost together. The group climbed free and headed for the stables. Crossing the stables would put them a lot closer to the main house. Somehow, they all knew.

"But I'm supposed to be the Paladin," Charlie said, dejectedly as they entered the relative shadow.

"Somehow, I don't think so, honey," Gloria said gently.

"But," Charlie began before being interrupted.

"Why am I even here?" Kelly asked, tears rolling down her face.

"Oh, suck it up, girl," Gloria scolded.

"Mom, you were just nice to Charlie, and then you're scolding me?" Kelly whined.

"Yeah, well, I've always loved him more," Gloria answered. She was half-joking. After that, they walked in silenced, Charlie taking the lead.

14

I Am Not Impatience

It took what felt like an hour for them to pick their way through the maze of secret passages and dusty hidden corridors. They climbed over plumbing that had obviously been added after the original construction. They had been forced to turn back twice due to what Charlie called Changes in the layout.

Indeed, the mansion was five times the size that any of them remembered it. Even Charlie and Jeffrey who had both seen old artists renditions and decades-old floor plans were amazed at its size. No lights were working, but the cultists had placed torches and lamps all throughout the house.

They had a few close calls with patrols. Several groups of cultists were moving from room to room searching. They had seen a great variety of dress among the cultists, seemingly from different locations around the world. Various items lay strewn all over the floors in every room and up and down the halls. The state of the house gave the impression that the searchers did not know what they were looking for, but that they were certainly determined to find it.

At the same time, many were not looking at tall. A large, loud dance party was underway in the main hall. Several hundred "people" were dancing to pipes and drums, what sounded like thousands of pipes and drums. Music was fast and loud, and the press of bodies was so close that the dancers moved more like waves of the ocean gyrating in unison than individual dancers.

At one point, Charlie led the group around the patio, which was full of dancers. Guards ringed the patio, making the small band keep their distance and crawl through the bushes. Fogged windows blocked the view of the party, but occasionally, the door would open, and the music became clearer, and they could see.

"What is this place?" Jackie asked as the group spread out into a concrete-walled, ten-by-ten room. A small two-tiered, like an end table, which Charlie almost immediately set the lamp on, and an old army chest were the room's only furniture. A chamber pot sat in the corner.

"Well," Charlie began. "I think it's some sort of bomb shelter."

"The ceiling looks like steel," Gloria observed.

"And it's thick too," Charlie said as he moved to an east wall and pointed out a handle built in there. "This is a shortcut up to Dad's inner office. Like the office behind the bookshelves?"

Everyone nodded; they understood except Jeffrey. None of them knew about the secret office, but by now, they weren't surprised.

"What?" Charlie asked, looking at Jeffrey.

Everyone turned to see the look of anguish on Jeffrey's face. He stood just inside the door at the base of the steps they'd come down. The pistol was half-raised.

"Are you just going to keep playing games?" Jeffrey's voice trembled slightly. "Give me the item. I will take it to Nero and make a deal."

Charlie edged forward with the bat in his hand, and a question frozen on his face. Everyone could see the gun still half-raised in Jeffrey's shaking hand.

"I can't wait any longer," Jeffrey pleaded. "We've wasted enough time already!"

"Just what kind of deal?" Kelly chafed.

"Wait, girl." Gloria stepped forward with her hand symbolically holding back Kelly and Charlie. "Something's not right here."

Everyone in the little room shifted positions slightly. Kelly cringed behind Charlie. Charlie raised the bat in front of him and stepped back as far as the small space and Kelly behind him would allow. Gloria and Jackie stepped up in front of Jeffrey. Jeffrey raised the pistol in a shaky hand and pointed it at Jackie's forehead.

"You're right about that!" Jeffrey spat, his face reddening, and a bit of spittle escaping his mouth. "You are wasting too much time."

"Why so impatient all of a sudden?" Gloria asked. "We agreed…"

"I never agreed!" Jeffrey snapped with a hiss in his voice. With a jerk, he pointed the gun at Gloria. "You all agreed! I was ready to go before! And I am not impatience!"

"Impatient," Kelly corrected at a whisper.

"Maybe I should kill one of you before I go as a gesture of good faith. Nero might like that," Jeffrey said in a contemplative tone. All the while, the look on his face was as if he had just unexpectedly bit into a lemon.

"He's possessed," Gloria said calmly. Then she closed her eyes consigned to the inevitable or maybe praying.

"That won't help you now," Jeffrey hissed.

"Stop!" Jackie leapt forward and grabbed the gun. The hammer closed on the flesh between her thumb and forefinger. "Leave us alone!"

Jeffrey let loose the revolver and crumpled to the floor unconscious. Jackie pulled the hammer of the revolver back enough to drop it and then crumpled to the floor herself. As she fell, she clutched at her belt. The room quickly filled with the smell of burning flesh. Acrid smoke rose from Jackie's midsection.

Kelly and Gloria rushed to Jackie's aid and helped her open her belt. Gloria grabbed the bowl and flipped it out onto the cold stone floor. It was hot, searing hot. But it wasn't red. Then when she flipped it off from Jackie, pulling some skin with it, it began to glow.

Kelly froze. Gloria was spewing foul language. Jackie lay on the floor half-conscious; her lower stomach felt like it was on fire. Out of one corner of her eye, she could see the bowl glowing brighter and brighter.

Jackie's hand fell on the bowl. It was no longer hot. She pulled it closer and gently fell sleep. The bowl's light had dimmed at her touch, and suddenly, everyone realized the crisis was over.

—◦◦◦—

"Being a follower of Christ is like being an invader in a foreign land!" Pastor Dan was shouting now. His face was red, and he slammed the pulpit with his hands so that it rocked under the force. "The enemy organization is elaborate! He has schemes within schemes. He has evil spirits that manipulate the minds of people even making them think thoughts that that are not their own, even making them think that those thoughts are their own! God's army only has one rank—Victor! When you signed up, you signed up to win!"

"But did you think"—he walked from behind the pulpit— "did you think that just because you joined the winning side that they—the enemies of God—would stop fighting?"

There were empty seats throughout the small sanctuary. It was only a week after Jackie had begun to follow Christ. She sat in the second row, listening and taking notes. Pastor Dan taught out of Ephesians.

That was the first day she had heard the words "spiritual warfare." She came to realize as he was speaking that the entire world had been involved in spiritual warfare. She started thinking of the events of her life, some less than easily explained as spiritual warfare. Everything started to make sense.

Then her vacation from work had ended. She had gotten busy and put the whole thing out of mind. Well, never completely out of mind. Pastor Dan had brought it up again and again. Jackie's mind became trained to detect when she was being manipulated without really trying at all.

"This war is not over!" Pastor Dan yelled. He was back at the pulpit now, and as he reached down for a sip of water before continuing, Jackie awoke.

15

The Moment

She was back on the cold stone floor, her abdomen still burned but not as intense.

Jackie looked around to see where everyone was. The room was thick with shadow. Gloria, Charlie, and Kelly were leaning over the table talking softly, and their bodies blocked most of the light. Jeffrey lay next to her with his face toward her.

She started slightly when she saw how close he lay. His forehead bore a swollen bruise. He must have hit his head when he went down. At first, he looked dead.

A single tear lay on the side of his nose, still near his eye. She rolled up onto her elbow. She shifted the bowl to her left hand and with her right hand, gently wiped the tear.

Just then, he woke. His eyes fluttered open, and another tear rolled down too fast to catch. He mouthed the words, "I'm sorry," and then repeated them with a soft rasping voice.

"It's okay," Jackie said, laying the flat of her palm on his cheek. "We are facing things here we do not fully understand."

He just nodded and then let his eyes go closed. He wasn't ready to get up yet. The pain in his head blocked rational thought. He struggled to consider what had happened.

Jackie cautiously rolled over onto her other elbow and tried to hear what the others were saying. After a few moments, Charlie noticed and moved to help her up. Glad to see her awake, they gathered around her.

"Thank God!" Kelly said sincerely.

"Yeah," Jackie said. "Do we know anything new?"

"Lots,'" Gloria said. "Some not so good."

"Seems like we're screwed," Charlie said. "The end of life as we know it. Doomed. Screwed."

"I know what screwed means Charlie," Jackie said.

Kelly punched Charlie in the arm. "Even if it's true, you don't have to keep saying it."

"Stop," Gloria scolded in her mother's voice. Then she turned to Jackie and began explaining, "According to your father's book, the Moment happens every so often throughout history. It's a God thing. Apparently, creation needs a rest. So it's like…taking time off."

"Except," Charlie butted in. Gloria gave him a stern look, and he stopped.

"Just let me explain, okay?" She turned back to Jackie, smiled briefly, and continued. "Except it never really ends. The only reason the others ended was because a group managed to overcome Nero. Your father was a member of a secret organization, which wanted to activate the bowl so that they would be the ones to face Nero next.

"According to the book, certain things always repeat during the Moment. Since there's no other way to tell time, it's sort of scripted. The space between events is called ages. They can be really short or really long. No one gets older here. No one dies except if they are killed. No one outside the Moment though. Everyone else is like frozen outside the story, and it's against the rules to hurt them."

"What about the children then?" Jeffrey asked, and no one responded in any sort of negative way even though this was the first they'd heard of him after his incident.

"Sorry," Gloria said. "It looks like they are the exception. Apparently, the cult can slay two specific innocents, and if they do, using the item, it's open season. The demons are free to kill anyone they want if the children are killed using the bowl."

"Permanently? I mean like forever?" Kelly asked. "I didn't understand that part."

"It just says for an age," Gloria answered unshaken. "It just says for an age and can kill anyone they want with no one to stop them. And it'll be a slaughter because they'll be defenseless, still frozen."

"What age comes next?" Jeffrey asked. "I mean after, if they succeed, I don't even know why I want to know but…"

"There isn't anything." Gloria laid her hand on the book. "Either it's never gotten that far, or the paladins didn't know about it. Don't you see? We activated the bowl. We started this, and we have to do something."

"Oh, we're going to do something, all right!" Charlie said and smacked the bat against the palm of his hand.

"Do we know what?" Jackie asked with tears rolling down her cheeks. Everyone was upset, but she was obviously taking it the worst. "What are we supposed to do?"

"This age is the age of searching," Gloria said in the tone of a tour guide. "Next comes the age of contact, the age of preparation."

"Preparation for what?" Jeffrey asked.

"For the age of contest," Kelly answered.

"What kind of contest?" Jeffrey asked.

"It looks like a horse race." Gloria stepped forward and put her arm around Jackie who was sobbing gently but deeply.

Why, God?

The next few silent seconds drew the little group together. Jackie stood in the center, and the others huddled around her. Jackie wept but did not crumble and finally asked out loud but in a gentle broken voice the question that any one of them might have asked, "Why, God?"

Kelly had long wanted to ask the same question. She had thought to ask it when she got a parking ticket or when she was late for an important date. She had wanted to ask God why when her father had died.

She had envied and then pitied her sister. She had envied her at first because she seemed to find meaning and purpose when she had become a Christian. Then the envy switched to pity when Kelly had realized that Jackie's life was not noticeably better. Overnight, Jackie had lost her ability to be genuinely sad. Jackie had seemingly placed her faith in a God that would allow all sorts of evil, even senseless violence. Jackie had begun to love him unconditionally and to believe that he loved her unconditionally even though the evidence did not merit that conclusion. Pity.

But oddly, not now. Kelly realized that in asking this one question, Jackie did something new and in a different way from what Kelly could have. Kelly couldn't bring herself to ask God why because she was afraid there would be no answer or worse, one she didn't like. Jackie not only asked the question she seemed to expect an answer.

Charlie's mind had been on the horse race. He'd thought about racing his whole life. To him, it had been his only dream. In the moment of his father's passing under mysterious circumstances, he'd put that away. He'd turned every facet of his being to solving the mystery that none else seemed to see.

Now here, he might ride for something so much more than a trophy or a purse. But he'd been pulled from his thinking, realizing his sister was in trouble.

Everyone here was in trouble. But Jackie needed some comfort, and over the years, he'd made that his job. So when she sought her comfort in God rather than in human support, he knew something was different. She clearly spoke to this "God" as if he were a friend and as if she'd been somehow betrayed. She wanted answers, and that made him want answers. Charlie found his curiosity peeked.

Jeffrey liked Jackie. Another time, another place and he'd have known exactly how to show it. Ordinarily, seeing a beautiful woman in distress, he'd have rushed to her aid. But her faith scared him, made him wonder whether she actually wanted him to rescue her and somehow whether she'd be better off without him.

Unable to resist his natural tendency, he edged closer and reached for her hand. He backed away though as she balled up her fists, pushed them down, tensed her muscles, and clenched her jaw. Eyes closed, she stood that way. Her posture said she wasn't going to move from that spot.

Jackie's posture and her desperate cry to God didn't pose a problem for Gloria as much as it did for the others. A mother's relationship with her daughter is different. Even though Jackie had changed in recent months and Gloria had rarely, if ever, said anything profound to Jackie, she loved her as only a mother does.

Gloria stepped in to Jackie. She gently grasped her biceps and softly said, "It's okay."

"No, it's not," Jackie said matter-of-factly without really opening her mouth.

"Okay," Gloria nodded. "You're right. It's not, but it is what it is. We have a chance here, Jackie. Hold on."

"It is what it is," Jackie said softly. Then she repeated the phrase over and over in her mind. On about the seventh time, it changed, and she didn't notice at first. She hadn't been counting, and her thoughts were so fast that she'd repeated the phrase two dozen times in a matter of seconds. The end was different from the beginning though. In the end, she was thinking, *It is necessary.*

Where have I heard that before? she asked herself. *The Word of God. The Bible.* As she worked through the following chain of thoughts, light dawned in the center of her mind. Many small nagging concerns hid from the light. These nagging concerns called out in everything from a figurative whisper to something like a construction worker's catcall. She ignored them and allowed the chain of thoughts to unfold, which it did very quickly.

It is necessary. The Bible speaks. Jesus had equality with God. He did not consider his equality something to be grasped He humbled himself even to death, even to death on on a cross. For that reason, God lifted him up. You too were once an object of wrath—works set aside for you to do. Take up your cross. It is necessary. I know the plans I have for you. It is necessary. A crown for the one who does not quit. Run the race to win. It is necessary.

Then nothing at all. Even the little thoughts that had been hiding and cringing from the light were now gone. The light that had come with the chain of thoughts remained but with silence and peace. She didn't understand the peace, but she knew it had come to stay. "I'm okay," she said.

Gloria could see in her face that she had relaxed. She let go of her arms and stepped toward the book.

"Are you sure?" Jeffrey asked. This time, he successfully snagged her hand.

She grasped his hand in both of hers for a second and answered, "It's gonna be okay. God's got this."

"I don't really believe in God," Kelly said. It was more of a reflex, said without thought.

"I know," Jackie replied. She let go Jeffrey's hand and took hold of Kelly's instead. Jeffrey didn't want to let go, but just at that moment, he was distracted by Gloria telling him that they had another problem. "I know. But you should, Kelly. You really should."

"It doesn't make any sense," Kelly said.

"It does actually. It makes perfect sense."

"How? How can you say that even now?" Kelly was getting a little angry, and it showed in her tone. "In the real world, there's enough evil. But look at here and now. Doesn't this prove that no loving God exists?"

"No, listen. Just the opposite. There are demons here. Like, don't you see? Demons are fallen angels or something. It more proves the things of the Bible than disproves, right?"

"We have a real problem," Jeffrey butted in. "Look."

Gloria held out the book. Jackie, Kelly, and Charlie, who had been lingering close together overwhelmed with curiosity about their own conversation, turned to gaze at a picture. The picture filled half the page and was hand-painted in. It was a cross on a chain.

"That's the cross!" Jeffrey said.

Gloria explained, "It says here that the Paladin needs the martyr's cross to be protected from the unseen evil influences that ally with Nero."

"That must be what hit you when we came down here!" Jackie blurted. "It was some kind of evil influence like impatience…"

"But that's really bad!" Jeffrey threw his hands in the air. "That's the cross! I don't have it! I sold it!"

17

Adam's Plan

In June of 1554, year of our Lord, time stopped, and the Moment began. Nero led the enemy. As was later discovered, the good Lord's plan, so circumvented as man has done, has other ramifications.

Though God declared a Sabbath and a holy peace, man had long ignored the command. The people of Israel again and again repented of their sins and turned back to God's ways. However, it seems that even in these times of supposed obedience they regularly overlooked the full implications of the Sabbath.

The full effect of this ignorance may never be known to me. But I now know, or at least believe, these things should not be separable for the man of faith. I believe that we have, by ignoring the commands of God, caused the Moment.

The earth soldiers on, never being given her proper times of rest. Man, society, nations, the ocean, even the stars need this rest. Man's sin is a tremendous burden for creation to bear. Then just as a man breaks down who soldiers on too long, it all breaks down.

Something in me wants to say that if man had known...if people knew the ramifications for ignoring the call of God to rest and reflect on him, to allow the land to rest, to allow the stranger who knows nothing of God to rest—but no. Because deep down inside, even those who do not know God at all have a yearning for relationship with him. God did say to Adam, in the day, that you eat of it, you will surely die, and Adam ate anyway. I do not think modern man would be any different.

A great gaping hole exists inside the soul of a man, and this is what drives us to consume all around us as if we believe that by consuming everything we can, we will somehow fill the hole. But the outcome of our avarice, of our covetous nature, of a lack of concern for the well-being of each other and our world...is the Moment.

For a time, all the activities of creation are suspended. Even death is set aside. For an instant, as it all begins, evil is free to destroy life, but that is gone before evil even knows it has come. Though they were free to destroy with impunity, they mostly missed their chance. It appears that evil, though lasting and determined, is not very vigilant.

No one knows when the moment first occurred. Reading Exodus, I have my suspicions. Only the ancient evil ones remember that it is coming again. Then there are a few who try to leave a legacy of record from century to century. What you now read is one such record.

In the Moment, the enemy is Nero. Where is Satan in the mix? I do not know. Nero is surrounded by demonic forces. They are organized, and they want nothing more than to complete the ritual. In so doing, they would be free to destroy defenseless humans all over the world.

For us, the Moment began when the chalice was activated. This happened by chance, providence, I'm sure, in a court of law. An impromptu trial marked by a profound spirit of confession, we now believe instigated by the chalice itself. We did learn that Nero could detect the chalice but did not know it was a chalice—presumably because it changes from Moment to Moment. The chalice activated, Thomas and Mary, Samuel Broadby's two children snatched, and the Moment began.

After that, nothing could stop one age from passing into another. In the Moment, time appears to have stopped in every other way, but progression of events is certain. Eventually, in what seemed like a day or two, even the sun hangs frozen in the sky, we stood face to face with Nero's court.

As I have said, Nero is for certain a demon, and there were others there as well. An ancient cult that has some pact with the demons was also present. These were humans from all over the world, no few died in the end, who were trying to aid Nero. I suppose they figured there was something in it for them.

Though at first I was quite angry, I now see that there was nothing else that could be done. When Sara, a consummate gambler, accepted Nero's wager, we advanced to the next age. Nero believed it was necessary as well. I think his evil cult would have overpowered Samuel, if with great losses. What's more, I know no reason why, other than the grace of God, a chance strike did not kill Rebecca, sooner leaving us defenseless against the demons themselves.

Our defense held out just long enough, and we formulated a desperate plan. There was no avoiding the contest, but our plan meant winning even if we lost. What follows are the details of the plan in hopes that the writing of it may benefit those who next face the Moment.

The preceding work was the largest surviving excerpt from the journal of Adam Black who was apparently the witness in the Moment that occurred in approximately 1554. The journal was rescued by the Paladins from a treasure horde taken from Luxemburg by the Nazis during World War II. However, at some point, the journal had been badly marred by fire, and only excerpts remain legible. Though substantial efforts were made by modern scientists at the time—circa 1950—no *further passages of value were recovered, and the details of what has been affectionately dubbed Adam's plan were lost forever.*

The above excerpt serves as hope that even if the team cannot win the contest, there may still be a way to overcome Nero. Notably, in the margin, Adam penned the words to a Christian hymn that would be written many years later, "My hope is built on nothing less than Jesus's blood and righteousness."

Many Paladins gave their lives to rescue these excerpts of Adam's journal. We hope their sacrifice will be justified.

Gloria put the book down. Two-thirds of the way to the empty pages at the back, she had to stop for a while. It felt like the middle of the night. Her back ached. Charlie and Kelly lay curled up on the floor, and Jackie and Jeffrey had been gone for what seemed like hours.

Apparently, time meant nothing here, but fatigue was still very real. She rubbed her eyes. "Are you awake?" she asked softly.

"Yeah," Charlie answered. "I'm beginning to wonder if sleep is possible here."

"Me too," Kelly said. She rolled over and sat up, rubbing her legs. "It's too cold to sleep anyway."

"It seems like they've been gone for a long time," Gloria said.

"No telling really." Charlie tapped his watch. The second hand slipped its catch and moved one second forward. Charlie waited expectantly to see it tick again but it did not. That little event gave him pause and made his mind wrestle with the concept of time frozen as if it were new again. And in any case, if as some think of it, "new" is defined by the length of time something has been—it was new.

"I told you we should have stayed together," Kelly said, pushing herself to her feet. She sat her feet side by side and bending at the waist, put her palms on the floor in front of her. It was the first stretch in her stretching routine.

"That's not helpful," Charlie responded.

"I've got some new stuff," Gloria said.

"Let's hear it," Charlie said, leaning back to crack his back.

"So there was this guy named Adam Black in 1554…" Gloria began.

Crawling

A veritable jungle separated the main house from the farthest southern track and stables. They were forced to navigate a maze of pathways marked here and there once they transgressed the boundaries of the modern day garden, by remnants of the city infrastructure.

In the farthest part of their journey from the main house, they were walking, not crawling among shoulder-high hedges. They had been walking since they had left behind the train crossing. At the beginning of the Moment, the train had just crossed a road now covered by grass and crisscrossed by hedges. The cars that had been waiting at the train crossing were engulfed in the foliage. The vines and bushes had grown over the train crossing. Even the train, which was only the locomotive, and three cargo cars long had the look of some great vegetation and steel kudzu.

Seeing the drivers of the cars frozen in place, in every case covered by leafy plants, damaged Jackie's calm. From there, Jeffrey's gentle tug on her outstretched hand kept her moving. She mumbled prayers to herself. She asked God to protect her, to protect them, and to guide the events upcoming.

They arrived at the rear of the bleachers that spanned the length of the track. Fifty feet high to the top row, they showed signs of particular care. Not a single weed rose among the steel support matrix. Clean, white gravel covered the ground. By and large, the bleachers were empty but in the lower rows…

Jeffrey led Jackie to under the bleachers where they had to stoop low to progress. From there, they looked out between the feet of spectators. Horses thundered around the track entering the final turn.

A dark gray mottled stallion led the way. He was three lengths ahead of the pack, which was composed of seven others. One rider, on a pale brown mare, was deep off the pack's pace by six lengths. The two interlopers watched with interest as the race concluded.

In the final seconds, a white stallion with a gray mane leapt from the pack and raced to neck and neck with the leader. Ten lengths from the line, it looked like a photo finish was imminent. Five lengths from the finish line, the former leader struck out at the new rider with his right arm, which in mid-swing became something like a long claw.

The rider of the white was ready and blocked the jostled strike with an upraised forearm that resembled a claw on impact. Three lengths from the finish, a fierce exchange of blows as parry and strike were lost in a blur. As the two horses crossed the finish line, the white stallion was in the lead by half a length but riderless. One of the blows had landed in the rider's midsection, and he had disappeared in a flash of burning embers.

Several hundred demonic cries rose into the morning air. Some were like shrieks of agony while others were bellows of victory. The bleachers were less than a quarter full. Only the bottom several rows were occupied. However, the volume of the noise at the race's conclusion rose higher than if the stands had been filled to capacity with screaming humans.

Jackie and Jeffrey clutched their ears, trying to block out the sound. To no avail though, the noise had some quality about it that struck them somehow internally. It shook the chest and pounded the heart. Fortunately, it was over as rapidly as it had begun.

It took what felt like an hour to cautiously work their way along the bleachers and peer up though the gaps at every feasible angle. They had to dodge patrols and sentries, buffeted now, and then by screams at highlights of four additional races. At the conclusion of the search, they were certain that the children were not in the arena.

19

Saul and Nero

The music was blaring in from the main hall. Nero slipped out of the writing mass of demon and humanity. The sitting room was quiet by comparison.

A single lamp burned on a low-lying table between a divan, and two chairs arranged for discussion. The sound of humming, low and melodious, was coming from the divan. Nero refreshed his drink from a decanter on a drink bar across the room in the relative darkness. "Need a drink?"

"It dulls my mind." The humming stopped but his first words carried a feint hint of the previous melody.

"I do think that's partly the point," Nero said. Nero moved to stand in front of one of the chairs across from the figure. Saul lay squarely between the arms rests of the divan. Even Nero, who carried a similar effect of his own, could not help but feel uneasy around Saul. Perhaps that was why they managed to get along—they made each other feel equally uneasy. Nero looked away. He contemplated how far his diabolical second-in-command could be trusted.

"Go ahead," Saul said, swinging up into a sitting position. "Go ahead."

'They're here," Nero said.

"You think so?" Saul asked.

"I'm almost positive."

"Almost?" Saul asked. Flippantly, he lay back down. That little doubt was enough for him. If they were here, Saul would hunt them. That was what he did. He hunted. He would hunt them halfway across the world if he had to. But if they were not within reach, he would go back to his melody. It was the only thing that calmed him.

"There is a blank spot in my memory. It's only a short time, but it's real." Nero drank the last of his drink. "Also…"

"That it?" Saul feigned, not caring.

"There was a broken window."

More not caring…

"Some said I broke the window on my way out. They saw me, but I don't remember."

"Wait a minute." Saul sat up and edged forward on the cushion. "And how long? How long is the lapse?"

"Moments." Nero liked Irony. Still it was lost on him this time how in the Moment where—if anywhere—time meant nothing, it suddenly seemed so important.

"So they are here." Saul jumped up. He pushed his palms together with force. "They are here. It is here. They have a Christian a-a-and…"

"Take your hands off of me," Nero interrupted. Saul in his excitement had grabbed Nero and lifted him to his feet. For a split second, the two well-dressed "men," who were not men at all, stared deep into each other's eyes. Neither saw anything but gaping emptiness, of course. Then Saul let Nero go and whirled around.

Saul pointed one toe at the floor and shot both hands into the air. He froze like that for a long dramatic pause. Nero thought he looked as if he had just finished a dance routine and was waiting for applause.

"They are here. They have the artifact," Saul said slowly.

"Yes, agreed."

"But they have a Christian, And he or she knows!" Saul's voice was full of kid-on-Christmas-morning excitement.

20

Garden Encounters

Jeffrey and Jackie rose to their full height. They stretched their backs. After creeping and crawling through their extended search, they pushed back against a row of eight-foot-high hedges and stood quietly. Jackie closed her eyes and raised her face to the morning light. Her fare skin soaked in the warmth of the sun, and she had to remind herself to stay back against the hedge and away from prying eyes.

Finally, Jeffrey broke the silence. "I'm really having a hard time believing all this."

"Hmmm," Jackie hummed softly, partly overcome by the serenity of peaceful garden.

"Jackie." His voice was a sharp hiss to get her attention. "Why are you so calm?"

"I'm not," Jackie answered without opening her eyes. "I'm barely hanging on."

"You seem calm."

"Maybe you should…" Her voice trailed off.

"What?" Jeffrey asked. "Should what?"

"Reality does not have to be believed. It just is. It is what it is."

"You think this all seems real?" Her beauty, the sunrise, the mist in the air, his own struggle with reality, his fatigue, and his frustration all combined to urge him to drop the conversation. Still, something inside him called for better understanding. "Flying beasts and frozen people. The sun is not moving for Christ's sake."

"Okay, listen to me." Her tone was somewhat scolding. "First of all, 'seems' is irrelevant. Real is real. Second, the sun does not move—the earth rotates. Third, some of the things we have seen here are more realistic than what we usually see…straight forward, I mean."

"What are you talking about?"

"Like the flying beast. He was a demon. I know it. It's just that we don't normally see them. That's all."

"I don't understand what you're talking about. Even if what you just said were true, why is it different here?"

"Weren't you listening?"

"What, to that crazy book? Half of what it says doesn't make any sense, and the other half doesn't help." He was agitated now for sure. His eyes were focused on her but not in her eyes, at her chest.

Not again, she thought.

Just then, a masculine hand with painted red nails shot out from around the corner of the hedge and grabbed her by the throat. Caught without her breath, she found herself face to face with a sinister-looking, dark-skinned, snarling man.

"I've got you now," he hissed through teeth carved to points. Smooth powerful motion swept her past him and slammed her shoulder blades into the ground. He came down on top of her, his knee across her collar bone and pressing on her neck.

Air rushed from her lungs expelled by the force of the impact. Spots burst before her eyes so that she almost missed Jeffrey's rescue.

Jeffrey pistol-whipped the huge man. The man simply turned and looked at him. Then with a snarl, the pointy-toothed assailant left Jackie on the ground, pushing off her throat so that she felt as if her larynx had been crushed.

As the massive native rose to his feet, Jeffrey landed a spin kick on his jaw. Jeffrey's heel dislodged several teeth but only forced him to turn his head briefly.

"Okay," Jeffrey said softly. With not much of a wind up, he booted the native's groin. His entire foot disappeared beneath the loincloth.

That seemed to work better. The native doubled over. Jeffrey grabbed his bald head between his hands and slammed his knee upward into the man's face. Another spin kick, this time heel to temple, and the man crashed to earth.

He landed on the grass next to Jackie. She had rolled over to all fours and was pushing herself up. The native groaned. His face was badly smashed and swelling rapidly. He struggled to roll over.

Muscular arms enveloped Jeffrey from behind. Jeffrey's arms were pinned down and leathery wings beat the air as the demon slowly hoisted him off the ground. He slammed his head back into the face of the diabolical newcomer, but to no avail.

"Freeze," Jackie croaked. Her throat burned, but urgency had rushed forth the word.

The beast's wings stopped beating, and both it and Jeffrey dropped three feet to the ground.

"Let him go," Jackie hissed. The beast's arms went limp, and he rolled his head back on his elongated neck as if howling at the sky.

Jeffrey turned on his heel and backed away from the beast. He leveled the pistol. He pulled the hammer back for emphasis. Jackie and the beast seemed to ignore him.

"Tell us where the children are," Jackie commanded. The beast cocked his head at the command and then in a flash, leapt into the air and flew away. "I had to try. Do you believe more or less, now?"

"Even less," Jeffrey answered. "And we gotta go!" He grabbed her by the hand, and they ran. The battered native had risen to his feet and snatched at them, but he missed and they ran.

21

I Want to Kill the Christian

"At the moment, we need them alive," Nero cautioned. Saul was standing at the patio doors. He had just retrieved his spear from behind the curtain there. He feigned checking its point. In reality, he was contemplating his course.

"At the moment, we need them alive," Nero repeated.

Saul bared his incisors at Nero and let slip a low rumbling growl. The gleam in his eyes spoke volumes about his distaste for being restrained. Slowly, his wings unfolded from his back.

"Saul, can you bring them to me?? Nero asked.

"She knows," Saul hissed through gritted teeth.

"And you are the greatest hunter to ever live. It may be a challenge but you should be able."

"I'd rather kill them and take the artifact."

"Of course. But if they don't have it or we don't figure it out or if God intervenes because we have changed the course of the ages? The ceremony is very precise. We could lose our chance."

"I want to kill the Christian."

"We all do. I'll make sure you get to if it's at all possible. But listen to me. So much more is at stake. We need the artifact and, if we win this, we'll kill them all. Do you hear me, Saul? We'll kill them all!" Nero was excited.

"I don't know."

"You can do this!" Then after a short pause, Nero decided to address the matter head on. "If we pull this off your past, our past failures will all be forgotten. We need this!"

"I swear God diverted my aim!" Saul snapped.

"I know! I know!" Nero grew tired of trying to encourage, but he was nothing if not tenacious. "I've never known you to miss with the spear, and of course, he was a man after God's own heart—maybe even then. It's not fair, but here it's our time. We make the rules except if we don't get the artifact, we cannot win. You see how David could have killed but chose not to, and he was honored for it. He manipulated things that way. Now we can too. Just long enough…"

"Jacob?" Saul asked softly.

"Of course," Nero said, opening the right half curtain to their fullest as he spoke. "He was a liar anyway. His name means that—deceiver. He was a God-bred, God-empowered deceiver. That's hard to overcome. No one really counts that against you. We've had this conversation before. Don't you remember?"

"The lesser spirits hate me."

"True. They envy you. None of them can lay claims like you." He stood face to face with the hunter whose own thoughts tormented him except when the music played. He looked deep into his eyes again. Their unifying trait was their hatred for God and all God's people." A long pause ensued during which both of them thought over their long history of failure in the many battles against God and his people. The thought of success must have crept in as well. The alternative to going on fighting was to accept defeat. To do so meant admitting God had been right. That could not be.

"We need that artifact," Saul said.

"Yes," Nero nodded. "Yes, we do."

Saul leapt from the patio doors. Beating his wings, he soared low over the garden. With the sitting room, he left behind the guise of a well-dressed man. His talon-tipped toes had always liked the coolness of the quickly passing night air. The predawn coolness of the Moment was equally pleasing.

Then he saw them—two humans, not of the cult, surrounded by demons and cultists. They were in the garden hedge rows. It appeared as if the fleeing quarry did not know that they were surrounded. For fifty heartbeats of a dying human, they fled this way and that trying to avoid the encroaching circle of foes.

The thrill of the hunt almost made him forget his conversation with Nero. If he had known for sure right then that one of the two was the Christian, he'd have struck. It only took a few heartbeats of a dying human to decide to stay up in the air and learn more.

Jackie's heart thundered. She led now. Pulling Jeffrey by the hand, she ran this way and that. Over and over again, the natives and demons blocked their way. The last several turns, she knew that they'd been spotted, and she began to suspect a game of cat and mouse.

Finally, the two mice stood at the near center of a large clearing. In its middle was a fountain. Three water bearers stood facing the center, their handsome faces and intricate stone waterpots a testimony to an artist's skill. Corralled, they stepped into the dry fountain bowl.

"It's over," Jeffrey said and dropped to his knees. He had said nothing during the last few turns of the chase, and just now, Jackie thought she knew why.

Two well-dressed men, four African natives, and one quite obvious demon approached from seven different directions. There really was no way out.

22

Gambling With Lives

Jackie started to feel a little hopeless and then rebuked the thought. *No time like the present*, she decided.

"You! Be gone!" Jackie stepped forward in the direction of the obvious demon and pointed and yelled.

The demon took to the air and fled immediately. However, he was replaced by a tribesman so that the way was not clear.

In desperation, she yelled, "All of you within the sound of my voice, in the name of Christ, I command you. Leave us alone!" The two well-dressed men turned and fled. They were replaced by tribesmen so that now there were seven tribesmen in all. The seven entered the clearing virtually simultaneously.

Jackie's shouted command had caught Saul up in the sky. He heard the command but reasoned that he was not included being unknown to her and far enough away, so he did not flee. The command freed Jeffrey who rose to his feet just in time.

On the first report of the revolver, the tribesmen changed demeanor completely. No more cat and mouse. They charged at their victims. Their squinty eyes, their battle cries, and their forward leaning posture showed that they were intent to reach Jackie and Jeffrey before Jeffrey's shots could halt their advance.

Jeffrey fired five shots in rapid succession as he pivoted on the spot. Three were head shots and took down their targets instantly. Two were chest hits near the heart, and their victims fell as well. The two remaining tribesmen crossed the low-lying wall of the fountain and lunged at their prey.

Jeffrey twisted out of the way and sent the brunt of the force of one of the flying tribesmen into the nearest water bearer's pot. Some of the stone crumbled, and the tribesman did not rise.

Jackie clenched her hands together and brought them up destabilizing the course of the next lunging tribesman. He landed more at her feet than on her. She stepped back and for no specific reason, looked up.

Just then, Saul was in the sky above her. She saw him and registered the look of approval on his face. Even though his face was gray and bestial and abnormally square, she could still see that he was enjoying himself. *Too much*, she thought. A loud and close shot rang out, and the tribesman crawling back to his feet in front of her dropped dead. She kept her eye on Saul. He chuckled when Jeffrey shot the tribesman.

The stone of the fountain basin made the spent brass ring as Jeffrey cleared the cylinders. The speed loader from his pocket fit six new rounds in place before another charge could be organized. Jackie began to think that there was nowhere to go. The outcome of the next charge felt certain and at the same time impossible. She knew there was no way that God would let it end here.

The tribesmen who had not charged were still lurking about. They could be seen sticking out from behind hedges here and there. Perhaps there were demons as well. Then she spotted another demon for sure on top of a semitrailer about fifty yards away. He had shiny gray skin and an elongated neck, and the morning sun made his left half appear orange. He looked strangely familiar, like the one who had grabbed Jeffrey maybe.

Saul drifted down gently into the clearing. He held his spear back and away. The smile was gone from his face, replaced by a look of great seriousness. "Don't send me away," he said when he had drifted down to a height where normal conservation could be heard. When he touched the ground, his talons were twenty feet from the fountain basin.

"I should," Jackie said, raising her voice slightly to cover a tremble.

"But please don't."

"One false move and you're out of here," Jackie said. As she was speaking, Jeffrey raised the .357 to point at Saul, but Jackie gently pushed it down. "Demon," she said softly.

"What do you want with us?" Jeffrey asked.

"I'll deal with the woman," Saul answered. "This is a conversation between celestial beings, Paladin. It's a thing you wouldn't understand. You are a good murderer. That is all. She has power, to her goes the glory when all is said and done. Compared to her, we, you, and I—we are but pawns."

"Is this what you want to say to us? You come to babble false praise and try to build up my ego while tearing down his?"

"On the contrary"—he moved in to about fifteen feet away—"I have waited a millennium to meet you. And you are everything I was hoping for."

"Enough!" Jackie said. "Just tell us where the children are!"

"That, I can not do," Saul said coldly. "However, if you will give me the...give it to me. I will take you to them."

"Give you what?" Jackie asked. She had just now confirmed that they did not know what the item was. She wondered if they knew what it was for.

"The knife," Saul answered.

Jackie shook her head.

"The medallion," he spoke again.

"Enough! No more guesses," Jackie chastised. "In the name of Jesus Christ, I command you to take us to the children."

Saul cringed at her speech, perhaps at the name of Jesus. Then after a second, he said, "You have great faith, Christian, if a bit misplaced. But I am forbidden until you agree to the contest. The rules of the Moment protect me."

"We agree to the contest." The voice was Charlie's, and he had just walked in from out of view. Gloria and Kelly were there too. "They let us walk right in," Charlie said.

"Of course they did," Jeffrey said softly.

"We agree to the contest," Gloria said.

"And the wager?" Saul asked.

"The artifact for the children as always," Gloria answered.

"Agreed," Saul said, and his wings unfolded. "But I want to hear it from her!" He stabbed one bony finger at Jackie.

"No," Jackie said simply.

"Or no deal," Saul snarled.

"Tell him, Jackie," Charlie urged.

"No," and again to Saul, "No!"

"She says it or no deal."

"No," Jackie said.

"You have an agreement," Charlie said and motioned to Gloria and Kelly.

"Your word means nothing!" He fluttered into the air.

"Neither does yours!" Gloria yelled.

"Fine then, prepare!" And he flew away.

"So do, do we get to see the kids or not?" Jeffrey asked in the silence that followed.

"I don't think so," Gloria said. "Somehow, I don't think so."

23

The Age of Preparation: From Contact to Contest

The Paladin

The Paladin in the Moment possesses the unique ability to utilize technology. Extensive research shows that this has always been true even though technological weaponry has not always existed. The term paladin is loosely applied since a paladin is supposed to be a holy knight—like a templar of sorts. In the Moment, the paladin is more often just a warrior with great heart.

The paladin is usually male and is an invaluable member of the team as in the moment there are always cultists somehow brought in by demon-kind. The paladin is uniquely equipped to deal with them. His combat skills are usually exceptional, and in at least two of the more recent Moments, he has shown an ability to activate technology, which at the hands of all others is nonfunctional.

The Rider

In every Moment we have recorded, the contest has been a horse race. Details contained in several sets of notes indicate that this may not always have been the case. For the present, day one would be playing the long odds to assume a contradiction of the horse racing trend.

Therefore, every member of the paladins has prepared himself with equestrian training. We believe that a properly prepared team of paladins might bring the cycle, which appears otherwise destined to repeat, to an end.

So then, the rider may be the single most important member of the team during the age of contest. Without the paladin to deal with the cultists and the witness to deal with the demons, the rider could not compete, but no rider means no chance.

The Witness

The witness is the real mystery for me. All accounts tell of the witness holding off and/or defeating demons by acts of faith alone. Of course, I believe in Christ, and I know the Bible tells of very real spiritual warfare that continues around us every day. I face temptation every day, and my faith seems to prevail. All of us want to believe, and we know that if we are chosen it may be as witness. That's a sacrifice we are prepared to make.

The Plan

The paladins train and prepare. We search for the artifact. It is always, by all accounts, an item used in some form of evil ritual. There has been a tome, a medallion, a knife, and a chalice (we think twice.) We have no real way to track the artifact although we know it responds to certain stimuli. In all of this, the paladins tend toward secrecy, which has as much worked against us as for us.

Along the way, and every paladin believes as far as I can tell, that the Moment could happen at any time we try to overcome evil. We work to gather more information, and we defeat evil at every turn. If an order finds and activates the artifact, overcomes Nero, and spares the earth, we may never know. On the other hand, if none do, we'll all be gone.

———— ❧ ————

Thick shadows and thin fog filled the stables. Only the small lamp lit the area where they rested. Gloria stretched upward to relieve the strain of hunching over the book.

Eerily, calm had settled over the little group since the challenge had been accepted. Gloria had read about such in another account of the Moment. With the heat off, imminent attack from the demonic forces theoretically forestalled, they all rested in relative comfort.

Jackie, Kelly, and Charlie lay in sleeping bags on the stables' floor. Jeffrey sat on a milking stool wedged up between a post and the wall. The pistol was in his hand, and he looked on edge except for the fact that he was asleep.

Gloria had placed the book back on the table where they had placed it when they had first come to the stables. She had been reading the whole time they slept. She was aching to share with them what she had discovered while they slept, but she wasn't sure how long that had been.

She tried to calculate the likely length of time based on her approximate reading speed and the number of pages she had read. That yielded something like four hours. Then she shook her head. The whole exercise meant nothing. Time was not passing, even bodily processes would be off. She knew from her studies that if they were not awakened, they would sleep without end. No matter how long they slept, they would awaken less than rested. She shrugged. What difference did it make then?

She decided to read a little longer. Her eyes were dry but not really tired. Her muscles were stiff but more from disuse than fatigue. She reasoned that the book seemed to rejuvenate her somehow. It didn't do that for the others; maybe that was the trainer's special ability.

A personal message to the trainer,

If the year of your Moment is prior to 2020 or so, the horse you want is called Black. I trust he will remain active at the beginning of the Moment, which should make him stand out. After my wife and my children, there has been no beast I loved more. He actually answers best to the name Coal. It seems he's been alive a lot longer than a horse should live. There is something supernatural about him. That is for certain.

At this writing, he is housed at my mansion. My last will and testament will be altered to leave my riches in trust to care for him. My son Charlie and my wife Gloria should be joint trustees.

I am certain that Coal has raced in the Moment before. The writing of a trainer named Jedediah thoroughly describes the horse ridden in that contest. Victory or defeat is unknown, but the spirit in the beast, if one and the same, says he is ready to race again. Even an inexperienced rider could complete the course on a seasoned horse. He was fully grown when my wife and I purchased him. It was my wife, Gloria, who picked him. She somehow knew immediately that he was special. He has outlived every horse we purchased after him, and though he has not raced, he has stayed fairly fit.

One more curious thing—the gypsy trader who sold us the horse called him a mare. At the time, I didn't really know the word. I thought it was simply another word for horse or stallion. I figured the actual definition some time later. The stallion is special. He and I have spent long hours—me talking and him listening—about matters of the Moment. If you find him, you will be able to get some additional information as I have confided in him secrets that should never be spoken.

At least one trainer has reported being able to speak with animals though it seems more like telepathy and limited to a horse's intellect. This may be just the edge you need. Find Black/Coal. I hope it helps.

—Charles

At reading the name of her now dead husband, and seeing the concern that he had felt toward the trainer-to-come, Gloria couldn't help but be touched. This had been his passion. The Moment had almost ruined their marriage, and he had never told her about it. He had managed to keep it from the many private detectives she had hired to follow him.

She half-smiled and shook her head, remembering several reports she'd received from private eyes who had said he had sat up late talking to a horse. She remembered shaking her head then too. She remembered thinking he had found out he was being followed, and that he had been playing games with her detectives to make them look foolish.

In those pages, she found new respect for the man she'd once loved. She was ashamed now of all the evil she had thought him capable of. A tear fell on the crease at the center of the book. She quickly wiped it out as best she, could and then wiping her eyes on her sleeve, she spun to look at the sleepers.

After a delay to watch for breathing, as a new mother quietly stares into her baby's crib, she pulled herself up and strolled purposefully toward Coal.

—∽∾∾—

Dreams don't come easy for a tired mind, struggling on the edge between disbelief and acceptance. Subconscious ravings try to clear fatigue, but in The Moment, the mind could not readily cleanse itself by picturing possibilities when impossibilities had become the norm. So broken dreams, more like the small strips of film, usually left on the cutting room floor, all pasted together, filled their heads.

Some aspects of what they had seen and encountered in The Moment were common to the dreams of all four unlikely heroes.

Demons, strong unexplainable feelings, and dark recesses breeched only by slivers of lantern light...

In Charlie's dream, Black is in the middle of the pack. Creatures resembling something he'd seen in a very dark comic book circle lazily blocking out the light of a predawn sky, a sound like war drums thrums in his ears. A cross, small but rising to fill his whole view blocks out all but a little light. A view lit by lantern light alone becomes a view of the book still in its wrapper pulled anything but fresh from the hole in the back of the stall. A splash of blood falls into a bowl of blood embossed with dragons, he whirls as a shot rings out, and birds fail to fly away. A man in tribal garb with a knife stalks two unsuspecting small children and the dream becomes even more a nightmare.

Kelly's dream is pain felt and pain seen replaced by blood on a little cross. It's Jackie's cross and the bowl looms large before her eyes. Images flash starting with Jeffrey's face sweaty and bruised and the gold-gilded pages of the book. Then a Bible lays open to Psalm 119, accompanied by tastes of fear and then the tiniest bit of salty water like tears and blood. The Bible is gone and Jackie is there and so angry. Everyone is angry and growing angrier. All the anger is directed at Kelly. She feels as if she is shrinking under the impact of scathing glances.

There is a horse race in Jeffrey's dream, and then suddenly Jeffrey is there in a race car firing an automatic rifle out the window at the jockeys. They explode on impact and the crowd's going wild. There's the finish line. Squirrelly little demons are all over the car. The hood is covered and visibility is blocked. Flames burst from the hood of the car.

Jackie's dream begins peacefully. As far as the eye can see, peaceful waves of tall wild grasses sway in the wind. The feel of a cool breeze and a warming sun gently overwhelms her, and then the sound of thundering horse's hooves and shouting breaks in. Two knights thunder toward one another, lances raised. They lower their lances to aim as they grow near enough. The tips cross and impact is imminent. Strong grasps and unwavering intention attempt to ensure accuracy. A great crash and blinding light erupt and in that instant Jackie realizes she is one of the riders, has been struck and unseated, and all is lost. She awakes.

Jackie placed her palms against the stables' floor and pressed. In this manner, she shoved herself to a sitting position, out of the sleeping bag, and then inched back until the column of stall number four supported her back. One by one, the others awoke while Jackie looked around, finding no gauge for the amount of time she had been sleeping.

Just then, Gloria strolled back into the little encampment. "Everyone well rested?" She asked, knowing very well the answer was no. She was leading Coal by the reigns. His saddle caught a random ray of light and glistened in its readiness.

"Did you stay up all this time?" Kelly asked. "Why are you so chipper?"

"No," Jeffrey groaned, hoisting himself to his feet.

Charlie stumbled toward the saddle. "Race time already?"

"No," Gloria answered, and her tone was almost scolding. "It's practice time. Get in the saddle. I'll walk you out. And as for the rest of us, no more sleeping."

"What?" Kelly began, but before the question could be voiced, Gloria went on.

"It doesn't work the same way here. According to Coal here—that's his real name—a little sleep, a little slumber, and ruin comes upon a man. The more you sleep, the weaker you get—so no more sleeping."

"That sounds familiar" Jackie put in "Like from Proverbs or something."

"But how long will we be awake?" Charlie asked, swinging up into the saddle. The leather creaked, and as he patted the old horse-turned-young-stallion on the side of the neck, he somehow began to feel more alert.

"According to Coal," Gloria dodged the posed question and answered the real one. "When we use our abilities, we will feel better. If we do nothing, we would eventually lapse into inactivity like the rest of creation. As for you, Coal says you have a lot to learn, and the two of you should be able to practice virtually without end so let's get to it."

"What about the rest of us?" It was Jackie. She had figured out that Mom was their new leader.

"This much I know. It's gonna be a while. You'll each need to use your gift to keep energized, to keep from falling asleep. The Paladin, Jeffrey's gift, is fighting, so try working out or sparring or something. The other gifts I don't know, but we've seen Jackie control them demon things, so something to do with that, and, Kelly, I guess you're just watching…Oh, and also the cross of the Martyr is big in this, so if someone could figure out something about that, it'd be good. I need to help Charlie get ready because if we lose the race, we lose everything. As Gloria strolled from the room, she left behind a mix of determination, excitement, and bewilderment.

24

What Kind of God?

Jeffrey immediately started thinking of ways to train while Jackie and Kelly looked at each other, wondering which one would fall asleep first.

"I don't get it," Kelly said softly so her mother could not hear. "What's my gift? What am I supposed to do?"

"I don't know," Jackie said. "I guess if you're a witness, you should just—watch. According to Pastor Dan, a witness is not only a person who sees but also a person who can convey what they see."

"Do you think the witness from the past Moments are the reason we have the information we do have?"

"Hmm," Jackie wanted to encourage her sister but knew that at least some had apparently come through a trainer. "Could be or at least could be this time."

Kelly found a notebook with nothing in it, and they went out to the bleachers to watch Charlie and Cole practice.

Kelly was determined to begin chronicling the journey in the notebook, but first, Jackie had something important to share.

Jeffrey practiced and did calisthenics in the stables at first. When the girls went out to the bleachers, he followed, telling himself it was because he didn't want to leave them alone, but in actuality, he had come to grips with the fact that he needed Jackie's protection.

At first, it was strange sitting in the stands watching Charlie and Coal gallop around the red stone track. True, the sun was stuck in the exact same positions in the sky for the whole time, and here and there, a flock of birds was frozen in place over head. There was a severed office building in the background against the multihued morning sky, and that was odd. What seemed most odd of all was that here and there dotted through the stands were other watchers.

The number of spectators watching what under others circumstances would have been a grueling practice varied with any given lap between thirty and forty. Jackie and Kelly sat close together, not exactly afraid, but wary. Jeffrey sat behind them with his pistol in his lap.

Gloria stood by the rail watching Charlie's every shift in posture. At the end of any given lap, she'd signal Charlie to stop or not; and every time he stopped, she had something to say. She even talked to Coal some, coaching him as well. Sometimes a spectator would pop in or out surrounded by a bit of smoke, but most times, they'd get up and walk away like an ordinary human. "I wonder if any of these are human…" Kelly said, voicing the thought that had just gone through Jackie's mind.

"Probably," Jeffrey answered. "It makes sense that there must be some more modern cultists somewhere."

"Maybe," Jackie said. "On the other hand, I'm thinking many things here are not as they seem."

"Such as what? I mean beyond the obvious," Jeffrey asked.

"Well, why are there no girl cultists? Why do all or at least all we've seen of the demons appear male? I mean, I know they're mostly covering up what they really look like but no females?"

"Right," was Jeffrey's only reply. With that, he drifted off into thought. He tried hard to remember a few Bible stories from when he was a kid. His grandfather had taken him to the local Baptist church Sunday school. Jeffrey had always been more concerned with the games and snacks, but he remembered his grandfather saying something like in the world, things are not often what they appear. Several thoughts drifted through his tired mind—of his grandfather and fragmented remembrances of Bible stories taught by people who seemed to be longing for bygone days when apparently, faith had made things happen. These thoughts as components formed a haze that kept his mind active while Jackie explained the most important mystery in the universe.

"God created the world," Jackie began.

"Right," Kelly said wondering where this was going.

"The first couple—Adam and Eve—were partly deceived and partly fell to their own selfish desires and disobeyed God. God gave Adam and Eve free will. They used it to sin against him. Everyone has free will to some extent, and God wants it that way. Evil finds free will quite useful for manipulation, leading to the sinful state of the world as people again and again choose to do what isn't right."

"It doesn't sound near as crazy as it used to since I have seen some of what I have seen. Still, even if the evil is real, that doesn't mean that God is real, or that he is who you say he is. Why let this go on?" Kelly asked. She was focused and listening unlike Jeffrey.

"If that were all you'd seen, I'd agree with you. If what we'd seen here were all we knew of God, I'd say okay. But it's not."

"Okay."

"You saw them flee from me. You saw them take my orders. Can you explain that?"

"No," Kelly said. "Unless…"

"Unless," Jackie interrupted. "God is working in me. When I gave my life to Christ, according to the way I understand it anyway, the Holy Spirit began to live in me."

Kelly scrunched up her face, indicating that something Jackie was saying wasn't sitting right with her.

Jackie turned toward Kelly and took both her hands. "Listen to me, Kelly. You know you've done things God wouldn't like, right? Call it mistakes or bad decision, wrong things, right?"

"Right," Kelly said. "I mean, of course."

Kelly looked very sad. She looked like she would cry. Jackie wanted to stop, but something told her, the Holy Spirit, she thought, that this was really important. So the Bible says that we can't go to heaven like that. We can't belong to God like that. We have to start over."

"I can't." She was crying now, not sobbing, but tears streamed down her cheeks.

"But you can," Jackie continued. "When Jesus died on the cross and came back to life overcoming sin and death, he made a way for us to do the same. You see? The restart? It's free. Paid for. All you have to do is accept it."

"I don't know," Kelly mumbled through lips wet with tears.

Just then, Jeffrey broke from his haze and saw Kelly crying. Rage, not from his own heart, rushed to the surface. "What are you doing?" he spat. "Stop this."

Jackie was stunned for half an instant and then responded, "Sit down and shut up." She commanded, and with robotic response that might have been comedic under other circumstances, he sat down and clasped his mouth shut.

"It's okay," she said to Kelly reassuringly. "If you can admit that you've screwed up and can believe that God loves you and wants you for himself, and you are willing to start living for him to the best of your ability, then Jesus makes it possible. Do you understand?"

"I think so, but what difference does it make?"

"Everything," Jackie answered. "There are only two sides. God wants you to be on his. Ultimately, you need to be. You were created for this."

"Okay," Kelly said, taking a deep breath and letting it out slow. "I know I've screwed up. I do a lot of things even I know are wrong. I don't know if they are all in the Bible or not, but I can't imagine God letting me into heaven like this. As for God, I can see he loves you. I don't know about me."

"He does," Jackie started softly.

"Wait," Kelly stopped her. "Because I can see he loves you, I can imagine he loves me. So I'm supposed to stop being what I've been and start being someone new?"

"Essentially, yes." Jackie was thinking Kelly would balk. She knew Kelly to be afraid of change. On the other hand, she had never known her to be this serious about anything. "But the restart that God wants to do in you, while like becoming someone new and awesome that God always wanted you to be, I think that you've always wanted to be…"

"Okay. Okay." Kelly stopped her. "Let me think."

Silence fell, and Kelly stared off into the distance. Her gaze centered on the skyscraper, and she found herself thinking, *What kind of God does that?* Events of her life, mostly hardship, came flashing forward into her mind's eye. *What kind of God allows that?* Soon there were so many thoughts in her head that she just wanted to say forget it all until later when she could think more clearly.

Then suddenly it was all gone. There was silence in her mind. One question remained—*What kind of God?* Kelly looked at Jackie. She bowed her head, muttering something, possibly praying.

What kind of God? Kelly asked herself. She scanned the stands. They were empty. No spectators remained. Jeffrey sat motionless; Charlie and Coal thundered around the track while Gloria watched on. *What kind of God?* She didn't know, but somewhere inside her, something yearned to know. She discovered that she had probably always wanted to know.

She pulled her hand from Jackie's grasp and laid it on her shoulder. Jackie lifted her tear-streaked face, and Kelly thought she read one last word on her sister's quivering lips—please. A deep breath again and knowing full well that she was going in over her head she said, "Yes, with all my heart, yes!"

"Oh, thank God." Jackie breathed and closed her eyes.

"Yes," Kelly said again, tasting the saltiness of her own tears.

After a short pause, the two of them prayed together. Jackie spoke a few words at a time, and Kelly repeated the prayer.

Jerusalem

Over Jerusalem, the cool air hung like damp moss on invisible strings of sky. Though you could feel the moistness and the thickness so that that at times walking felt like pushing through wet blankets, what held the air in place was invisible to the naked eye. No meteorologist had ever forecast this.

It was as if the humidity were at or above one hundred percent, but instead of clouds and rain, there were clinging patches of moisture. Then the sky was hazy like fog but clear enough to make out the late evening sun. The shadows of the taller surrounding buildings made the narrow street seem cloaked in darkness as if night had wrestled with day and somehow held its own.

As Jackie's foot touched the ground, the reality of the Moment hit her again. The mystery of the world was new and fresh here. They had raced to the complete opposite side of the world at speeds one should not travel without a helmet, a body armor suit, and certifiable insanity. The Moment remained. The dimness and dampness made the place seem as if it were an extension of where they'd left. The ringing in her ears from the rushing air and the smell of sulfur in her nostrils reminded her of the grueling ride. So they were in Jerusalem.

Coal removed himself to a nearby rooftop for reasons of his own. Jackie glanced at Jeffrey out of the corner of her eye. He was sneaking a glance at her in just that second, and they silently agreed to proceed.

Outside the Moment, the street they were walking down was obviously bustling with activity. Now no one else was moving—all were suspended in inactivity as all the people back home had been. Jackie and Jeffrey had to slip sideways between pedestrians. Thousands of pedestrians filled the street. Almost every single person appeared to be headed somewhere with purpose but was going nowhere at all due to the inactivity of the Moment.

As Jackie and Jeffrey rounded the corner, they were stunned by what they saw. The midsection of the street was engulfed by a frozen ball of flame. The ball consumed the middle third of the block, and even as they surveyed the scene, some members of the pedestrian crowd were swept from their feet or bathed over in rolling fire and debris. They crept forward entranced by every detail.

Metal, wood, and glass fragments had already flown into the crowds. One man cringing with his arms over his head and fear on his face was frozen in place as a jagged piece of glass protruded from his forearm and forehead.

"Can we," Jeffrey started and then as he stopped near a petite oriental woman crouched over a young girl he finished. "Can we move them?"

"Let's try," Jackie replied moving quickly to grab the little girl.

Once they realized they could move the people in the path of the explosion, it took some time to move them all. They estimated a safe distance—that was the best they could do. When they were all but finished, it occurred to them that the other side of the exploding shop had almost certainly faced a street as well, and it took a while longer to complete the process on the other side. In the end, they had moved hundreds of people who would be very surprised, confused, and grateful when and if the Moment ended.

During the second round of saving, they discovered another problem. The exploding shop was the one that they had come for. The name of the shop, stencil-painted onto a flat wooden sign, was mostly unseen behind the ball of fire that jutted at odd frozen angles from the shop's shattered windows.

However, on the back side of the shop, they figured it out while moving one of the patrons. The lady was carrying a partially melted shiny plastic bag with the words Gamaliel's antiquities still showing. So after everyone had been moved and a smattering of first-aid had been applied, they stood in the cleared street staring at the shop.

"How do we get in?" Jeffrey asked, more thinking out loud than expecting an answer.

"The fire is very hot. Even frozen like that, I couldn't get close. Also, the air right around it is, well, like, odd."

"What do you mean?"

"I didn't like touch it, but I could tell it was hot. And I got a really funny feeling, like pulled or something," Jackie explained.

With a thoughtful tone, Jeffrey began, "Here's a thought. The fire is frozen, right? It's not really burning anything. So couldn't we just rush in, get what we need, and rush out. Even if it hurts, we should be fine when we come out, right?"

"Uh, I don't think so. Besides, how would we see if the whole place is filled?"

"Good point."

"We could find some fire gear, like at the fire station," Jackie began and rotated on her heel, scanning up and down the street to see if one caught her eye. "But then…we still couldn't see." She stopped scanning.

"What about water? Or a fire extinguisher?" Jeffrey asked.

"No water pressure really. Although otherwise it might work. A fire extinguisher might too but it probably wouldn't spray."

"It might for me," he said, strolling toward a nearby shop.

Jeffrey returned with a fire extinguisher and found Jackie by the fire near to the front door. As he approached, she held up a fragment of wood. "Check this out." She held the wood up, and it was sucked into the fire and disappeared.

"Yeah, when you get close, you have to be careful because it's pulling."

"But that doesn't really make sense. It's an explosion. Shouldn't it be pushing?"

"I'm not sure. I mean, fire consumes but explosions explode. I don't get it either."

"Well, anyway, can't do any harm to try spraying it, right?" Jeffrey readied the fire extinguisher he had borrowed. Jackie simply shrugged and stepped away.

Jeffrey aimed the extinguisher at a spot nearly in-line with the door knocking down some debris with the extinguisher's nozzle before squeezing the release.

"I don't think it's going to work," Jackie said.

"Oh, ye of little faith."

"Not really," Jackie answered too soft to be heard.

At first there was nothing. Then a sputter and the extinguisher sent white foam jetting through the fire.

The two of them stood amazed at the results. Jeffrey had only released a burst of a second or so, and yet the jet of foam cleared a path fifteen feet, toward the door. The path was far wider than it was deep, chopping off the majority of the front of the fire and narrowing as it approached the door. Bits of broken glass, wood splinters of varying size, and a light layer of white foam covered the ground along the path.

"That worked," Jeffrey said swallowing hard.

"Too well, I'd say."

"Yeah," Jeffrey started slowly forward down the path. Jackie tagged along behind realizing now that they were actually walking down a ten-foot-high tunnel in the flames.

"I don't think science works the way we think it does," Jackie said with a hint of nervousness in her voice.

"At least not in the Moment anyway," Jeffrey replied.

The extinguisher carved a larger than necessary tunnel in the flames until they reached the main show room of the little shop. The foam knocked down lots of flying debris so that they were forced to step over mounds of foam-covered bits and pieces to get in.

26

Inside the Fire

In the center room of the shop, they could see by the orange hue of the fire that remained all around them. Even with the air cleared of flames, the air all around them was so hot as to be almost unbearable. A cool breeze wafted in, maybe the first they'd felt in the Moment, replenishing the stale, oxygen-deprived air. Soon enough, the breeze stopped; and though the air became more breathable, it remained hot.

A satchel appeared the source of the explosion, and a grotesquely disfigured man hung in midair. Jackie and Jeffrey kept their backs to the disfigured man as they scanned the showcase. The glass in the case had all been broken.

"Here," Jeffrey said, reaching into a case.

"Wait! It might be hot!"

The two of them stood peering into the case, Jeffrey sucking his singed fingertips. The air, or at least the staleness and hotness of the air, made it hard to breathe. A two-by-three-inch placard lay askew from its place, surrounded by fragments of glass. It read Cross of the Martyr, but the word *martyr* was written in funny script so that the word looked like m-a-p-t-y-p.

"Cross of the map tip?" Jackie asked incredulously.

"It must be Greek or Latin or something for martyr. I think I've seen it before," Jeffrey answered. He had pivoted and was looking for something to use to pick up the cross. He thought he saw a glimpse of movement outside in the courtyard, past the mouth of the tunnel.

Suddenly, he realized the whole thing was a trap. He choked out the words, "The cult," as a wave of emotions hit him.

Clearly, they had set off the bomb to destroy or conceal the cross. The cult here knew so much more about the Moment than they did. It struck him as being like playing chess against a master without even knowing all of the rules. Suddenly, it became clear that the outcome was certain. "Trap," he croaked as his knees buckled, and he knelt under a great weight like that, which he had seldom known. In ten seconds, he had gone from looking into the case to kneeling on the floor head hung, shoulders slumped.

Jackie turned from the case. She saw Jeffrey fall sideways and go into a fetal position. Her first thought was the heat and lack of oxygen in the place. The word *trap* hung in her mind, however. That was just enough as a robed man in a dark turban charged her, his mouth open in a silent scream.

She leapt to the right, and grabbing at his clothes, she gave him a shove to help him by. He bounced off a showcase and disappeared into the fire. That left her back to the tunnel, and a second assailant grabbed her.

He clenched a full hand of her hair and wrapped his other hand around to bring a ten-inch dagger to her throat. She caught the dagger arm with her left hand and his upper arm with her right and tried to flip him. He twisted her head back hard, and the flip failed. She shifted both hands to the dagger arm and slammed her body backward so that the man slammed into a pillar in the center of the open area.

She had the strength to hold off the dagger arm two-handed, but she knew if she let go with one hand, he'd plunge it into her. He was pulling her hair back and down so that she stretched to reach. Two more cultists picked their way through the tunnel. These were dressed the same as the first two but the front one carried a wicked-looking dagger.

A House Divided

Saul drifted down through the sitting room window. His leathery wings folded back and disappeared as his talon-tipped feet touched the floor and transformed into shiny shoes. He retained his spear in his left hand as he scanned the room for Nero. The ancient markings on the spear contrasted his trim, black tuxedo. Still, he considered himself on the hunt and so, would keep it near.

"I am here," Nero said, advancing from the shadows and smoke beyond the roaring fireplace. The smoke was an effect of the moment more than from the fireplace, which burned hot and bright.

Saul crossed the room to stand near Nero, and again they stood face to face. "They prepare for the contest, but we have a problem."

"Yes, I know," Nero replied.

"Of course," Saul said. His anger seethed inside him. The lesser spirits were always stealing his thunder. They were fond of Nero, and he was pretty sure, actually worked against Saul at times. He suspected they all envied him and wanted favor from Nero who could probably allow them to manifest under the right circumstances. Nero's welcoming the lesser sprits had made a mess of his mind but had never been anything but an advantage as far as Saul could see.

"What's our next move then?" Saul asked.

Nero knew that Saul's loyalty only went so far. Still, he was Saul's commander, and that skill set clicked on at the request. He had been deep in thought trying to remember the details of past moments. He had been asking himself whether this problem had occurred in past contests. Now he was as ready as could be to answer the question. "We must harvest a rider—a tribesman who can ride better than their rider. All the ranks must rally to do this. Put them to the test, and give me the best the world has to offer."

"Yes, my lord." Saul had a bad feeling that things were slipping from his grasp. "Of course, it will take time."

"That we have. Search the world. Find me a non-demon rider who can ride our best nightmare to victory in the contest. Better yet, find me ten. We will field them all as is our right. Make sure that they know which one is the best, and that they are to aid him to win. Also, they must ride for fear of their lives. No rider has ever ridden faster than when he is in fear for his life." Nero squeezed his fist tightly and spoke the whole of his commands across his knuckles.

"The demon riders will not be happy," Saul cautioned.

"They will do as I command, and they will like it! If they want any chance to win and have all the humans to kill—to kill all the humans—they will do it." Nero turned now and peered into the roaring fire.

Nero's pupils shrank to nearly their smallest size. A thrill of warmth spread through his members as he peered deep into the fire's ever-shifting recesses. "Perhaps we will burn them all…" His voice trailed off.

Saul shrugged. He turned toward the window to carry out Nero's orders, but just as he was about to transform, Nero stopped him.

"Saul?" Nero called.

"Yes, my lord?" Saul answered without turning back.

"Let the demon riders assess the cultists. Let them pick the best. That should help ease their discontent." With that, he added another log to the fire even though it threatened to escape the fireplace at its present size. "Don't worry about the Christian and her friends. Fear and doubt will keep them busy until we are ready."

"As you wish," Saul said. He did not like the idea of leaving such an important task in the hands of two lesser spirits even if they were two of the best. He leapt through the window transforming in flight. *No more orders,* he thought. *No more.*

As he flew, he thought through his next move. He knew that now was not the time for an open power struggle. He was certain that this time, this moment was the best opportunity they had ever had to overcome God. He had to get the object. If he had the object, he could make his move.

If the chosen children were sacrificed, they'd be able to kill every human, bring an end to this whole ugly business, and prove God wrong once and for all. But if all that happened on Nero's watch, he'd be insurmountable.

Saul had to find a way to get the object and sacrifice the children himself.

Still, Nero was formidable, which would make token allegiance a continuing necessity. Plus, by now, Nero might know what the object was. The lesser spirits would have been watching the quarry. If they had learned what the object was, they would have shared that information with Nero. If Nero knew what the object was, why didn't he just overwhelm the quarry with cultists and take it? Deep inside, he knew that there was another reason not to do it that way, but he couldn't remember what it was.

He tried to think back to past attempts but could not remember. That made him tremble. He knew that only one power in the universe could do that. Only one power in the universe could make him forget, could overcome his mind. That secret plagued him, and his lack of memory stirred up his hatred for God. The lost information had to be the key to everything. Otherwise, he would remember.

Then it hit him. Just as he had finished delivering the orders to the riders to search the world for the best cultists to ride in the contest, standing at the track, where moments before demon riders had raced in preparation for the contest, it hit him. It hit him as he watched them soar off into the sky in dozens of different directions on their nightmares, and the nightmares hooves burst into flames and then their manes, and then they were gone. In that moment, it hit him.

Saul thought about the book. The three humans who had shown up last in the garden had known something about the age of contest. And the woman had been carrying a book. That's where they had gotten their information. It was not the object. Of that, Saul was almost certain. But in past moments, God had always provided a way for a trainer among the quarry to figure out what was going on. And if the book could educate her, maybe it could educate Saul. With that realization, he took to the air and set his course for the stables where the human prey had been staying.

A melody found its way to his lips, calming him internally. A boy, playing a harp, from so long ago…but this boy did not play like a boy. He played like a king. Saul tried to shake it off. It calmed him nonetheless. He resolved he would get the book.

28

One Escape and
One Failed Escape Attempt

"Jeffrey!" she cried. She thought she heard him moan. "Oh, God, help me please!" She spent most of her breath on her prayer, and she thought she heard Jeffrey moan again.

Meanwhile, the cultist coming down the tunnel could see the situation in the room and broke into a run. "Infidel!" shouted the spearman.

Suddenly, she knew what she had to do. "In the name of Jesus Christ, I command you to be gone!"

"Die!" the cultists who held her hair yelled.

"Not you! Leave Jeffrey alone!" she yelled again. Jeffrey sprang to a crouch and then rose straight to his feet. The move only took a fraction of a second, but it seemed like an eternity to Jackie wrestling over the dagger.

Jeffrey dodged the first thrust of the spear and fired the .357 point blank into the face of the cultist. The cultist froze and fell while the high-powered round exited the rear of his skull and impacted the cultist behind in the neck. He dropped his sword and tried to staunch the blood flow but could not and fell.

Jeffrey spun on the cultist holding Jackie. The cultist jerked Jackie's head back up in front of him so that he was protected from Jeffrey's aim. Jeffrey promptly shot him in an exposed knee.

The cultist twisted back on impact, and Jackie slipped from his grasp. One more shot from the .357 surely killed the cultist although he was sucked up into the flames so that they did not see the impact.

Jackie picked up the dagger from the cultist and used it to remove the cross from the case. "Thank you," she said.

"No problem," Jeffrey answered. "Sorry about that first part there. I just couldn't breathe for a minute."

They left the shop. Coal met them on the street. Jackie wasn't ready to mount up just yet. *There might be no better time*, she thought.

"Jeffrey," Jackie began. "Who's God to you?"

"I guess he's the man upstairs," Jeffrey answered. "He's the one who made everything."

"Is that what you really believe, or are you just telling me what I want to hear?"

"I believe it. I guess I always have, but I've been real angry at God." He held the reigns stroking the rough leather with his thumb but did not move to mount, sensing this was going somewhere. He gauged Jackie's look of concern and then shrugged. "Some *Christians* essentially stole my wife from me." A sarcastic tone slipped into his voice when he said the word Christians as if to say that he knew they were not what they said they were.

"Even Christians can do wrong things in the name of what they think is right—if they even were Christians, and in any case, it doesn't mean God wants it."

"Listen." Jeffrey let go of the reigns and turned toward her completely. "Here is what I don't get. Either God's all powerful and in charge or he isn't. Do you know what I mean?"

"Oh," She said. "Right, I had that question too. But here's the thing. To love, people have to have free will. God can't or at least, won't take it away. He loves us, and he wants our genuine love back."

"Well." Now there was anger in his voice. "There's his mistake. First of all, some people don't deserve it, and second, some use theirs…free will I mean…to abuse others. They should be stopped."

"He will, in time."

"Not fast enough." Jeffrey turned back to Coal.

"People need time to believe." She was searching for the right words.

"Well, while he's taking his time, let's get my son back, shall we?" He swung up, signaling the conversation's end. As they rode, Jeffrey was angry, but at least now he was angry at the people who had taken his wife and his child rather than at God. He couldn't do anything about the people who had taken his wife, at least not until this whole mess was over. He could do something about the people who had taken his son. He was going to make them pay!

29

The Secret to a Successful Appeal

Charlie wasn't tired at all. He'd ridden for hours and had learned a lot, but when Jackie and Jeffrey had taken Coal to go look for the cross, he'd been ready to ride a lot more. He'd even suggested that he take one of them, but Gloria said no. According to what they knew, the two of them would need each other for protection.

What's more, Gloria believed that the others would be safe for the moment. During the age of preparation, there should be no conflict. That of course meant that it was the perfect time to be looking for the children. So Charlie paced around the stables while Kelly watched and Gloria researched something in the book.

"Charlie, c'mere," Kelly said.

"I just can't believe we are wasting all this time!" he replied as if she'd been questioning his impatience.

"It's okay," She said. "The race will come soon. Fretting over it won't change that."

"Who are you, and what have you done with my sister?" Charlie half joked. Both of them knew that Kelly had been anything but calm at times like this. She should have been hysterical, sobbing, or throwing a fit. Still, she looked at him calmly and motioned to the bench next to her.

"I need you to listen to me.

"All right," he said. But as soon as impatience was gone out of him, as soon as he felt the wood of the bench on his rear, he felt the grip of fear on his heart. She started talking, but he wasn't hearing her. All he could think about was how important this race was and how he was likely to lose. He needed more practice, but even with the notion of practice, the question of whether he could ever be good enough plagued him. Every failure of the past piled on him as if it were new again. The cold grip of fear of failure tightened around his heart.

"Charlie!" Kelly scolded him. He promised he'd listen at that but went right back to his cluttered mind until three sentences later, she caught him obviously wrapped up in his thoughts and scolded him again. "What is it?" she said this time.

"Seriously? The fate of the world rides on the outcome of this race, and I'm the world's rider!" He spit it out all in one breath and with an incredulous tone.

"It's going to be okay," she said.

"How can you be so sure?"

"And I don't think the fate of the world rides on this race." She was pretty sure that was true now that she had said it although that was the first time she had thought it.

It didn't matter because Charlie didn't hear it anyway, lost again in fear of the future and doubt of his own abilities.

"Stop," Kelly commanded. "Be calm!"

Immediately, Charlie felt better. He stopped wringing his hands, stopped fidgeting around on the bench, and the urge to run left him. "What?" he asked quietly.

Kelly closed her eyes and prayed, *Jesus, help me.*

"What?" Charlie asked again, growing a little impatient, contemplating, shaking her to get her attention.

"In the name of Jesus, I command, I command you to leave, to leave him alone. Go away, go away, and forget the way back." Her voice was faltering but not because she was afraid. It was faltering because she was trying to find the words. She wasn't sure of herself. She was sure about Jesus; of him she was certain indeed. After a second, she said, "Better now?"

Charlie said nothing but nodded yes.

"Charlie," Kelly began, suddenly feeling a bit exasperated. "We are dealing with things outside our understanding here."

"Ya' think?" Charlie quipped.

"Listen," she chided. "I don't know how, but I know this whole thing is about Jesus. You understand? It's about Jesus."

"I don't know." Charlie was shaking his head.

"When I was talking to Jackie before somehow, we figured it out. I mean, we are all screwups, ya' know? Because of that, we deserve what we get, and this might be part of that."

"Okay, I'm buying the screwups thing, but this is part of that? What does that even mean?"

"Okay, I mean, we do lots of things that are wrong, and that can't continue forever, right? I mean eventually, there has to be a sorting out. Like a judgment day." She was praying in the back of her mind and wishing to switch places with Jackie and knowing that this was the best opportunity to talk that they'd had, might ever have.

"So this is like judgment day, like you always hear about? Not exactly what I expected." Charlie's tone was still doubtful.

"More like avoiding it, I think." That stopped him in his tracks. He could see that. If the race were lost and the world were open to the hands of these demonic enemies and if they were as plentiful as he thought they might be, then that would be like judgment day. Yeah, he could see that.

"So maybe this is like one last appeal?" He was formulating an understanding. He'd had a year of law school. No one who has ever studied law is completely without the understanding of a higher power with a greater sense of justice than men could emulate.

"Okay," Kelly said. "Maybe like that." *Where to go next?*

"So we lose the horse race, we lose the appeal."

"Maybe. Maybe not," Kelly said. "I'm trying to tell you. If God is real, and I don't think that's an if, but just to say it that way, if God is real and judgment is real, then why not salvation and think about the demons and how Jackie can send them away."

"So you are saying that Jackie can do what she can because she claims to be a follower of Jesus Christ?" The incredulous tone was creeping back in.

"Not just claims to be. She is one. And..." Here went everything. She had to lay her cards on the table right now, even if it meant that he would stop listening to her. "So am I."

"You?" Charlie questioned, "Jesus? I mean…you and Jesus?"

"You say it like we're dating, but I mean to say I have given him everything. Everything."

"Seriously? What about alcohol and partying? Staying out all night with your friends? What will your friends say?"

"Hey, whose side are you on any way?" She paused and put her fingers to his mouth. "Brother, I don't have all the answers, but this much I'll say, if God wants me to never touch another drink, I will never touch another drink. If he wants me to go to bed by six every night, I'm there. I will tell every person who will listen, including my so-called friends and my bratty brother 'cause I am not ashamed. You hear me, Charlie, Jesus is real. He died for me, he loves me, and I love him. I love him so much that I now understand that I may never have loved anyone or anything else in the world, ever! I need you to believe me. I need you to accept what I'm saying. If we believe in Jesus, we win this thing, guaranteed."

"Okay, little girl," He said, slowly removing her hand and cradling it gently in his own. "Okay, so if we believe in Jesus, we win the race, right?" She started to shake her head. "I believe you. I believe you. I'm just trying to figure it all out. So if we believe in Jesus, we win the appeal?"

"Yeah, I think that's it." She could see he was taking her seriously. She could see that maybe he was weighing it out. "Believe, Charlie," she said very softly under her voice, and then she asked God in her mind to carry it home.

There was a long pause. It may have been two to three minutes if time had meant anything. It seemed much longer to both of them. At last, Charlie broke the silence.

"I'm going talk to God now," he said. "God, it's me, Charlie. I know it's been a long time. I just want to say that even though everything I'm seeing around me seems to speak pretty badly for the way you've set things up, I guess you've got the right. I mean, I know I'm a screwup, and I deserve maybe even worse than this. I'm real sorry. Anyway, I guess you sent Jesus to die for us just like they told us back in Sunday school. I really didn't know. Anyway, this is me believing, and I'll give you whatever is left of my life, even though it may be only this one horse race. And um, as for the rest, I'm leaving that up to you, okay?" Then there was a little more silence, and he felt a tear roll from his nose, and he opened his eyes to see Kelly beaming, from ear to ear, a smile. "Okay?" he asked her.

"Okay," she said.

30

Thievery

Gloria heard a noise and got up to walk toward the door of the stables. Charlie and Kelly were facing off with a single "man" in a pinstriped suit. She picked up a pitchfork and strode forward. She was thinking that without Jeffrey, this could go poorly.

"My master Zephyr wishes to come and talk to you," he said. "He wishes that you will not send him away." The man had a distinctly Brooklyn accent. "He just wants to say something to you, and that is all. It will only take him a few seconds. Okay?"

Kelly and Charlie looked at one another. They weren't sure, but they decided to agree. The man walked away. A beastly demon swooped in to take his place. He stalked forward on his talons until he stood twenty feet away or so.

"That's far enough," Kelly said authoritatively.

"Where is the other one?" the demon asked. "The first one?"

"Doesn't matter," Charlie answered. "Speak your peace."

Upon Charlie's command, the beast looked him right in the eye. A look of surprise crossed the demon's face. "I see. It spreads like a plague. Be true! Be true to what you say. That is all I say to you! I have known them true and found them false as well. Be true!"

"Is that what you came here to say?" Charlie asked.

"No." The demon rolled its head on its elongated neck to take in the sky and then once again peered back at Charlie and Kelly. "Tell her. I can wait no longer. I have done my part. Do you hear me? I have fulfilled my obligation. Do you hear me?"

"Yes," Kelly answered. "But what oblig—" She stopped because the beast was gone.

"What do you think he meant?" Charlie asked.

"By which part?" Kelly asked.

"The part about fulfilling an obligation."

"It sounded like they had some sort of deal." Kelly was more thinking out loud than answering, but Charlie took it as an answer anyway.

Meanwhile, Gloria looked back to where she'd left the book. She saw it wasn't sitting where she thought she had left it, and concern rose in her. She dashed to the table. She scanned the area, hoping beyond hope that she had set it aside. Nothing there, she called for Charlie and Kelly.

The mood in the stables was impacted harshly when they returned to find that while they were dealing with their visitor, someone had stolen the book. The lantern was still there, so whoever stole it, did not know what they were doing, but it was a heavy loss nonetheless.

"So it was a distraction then." Charlie said. "Now what?"

"That's a good question," Gloria said. "I guess we wait, but we may have a real problem. There could be something in there yet that we really need."

"So are you suggesting we go try to find it?" Kelly didn't like the sound of it. However, she was getting past her fear, and waiting didn't sound very appealing either.

"No. No way," Gloria said.

Kelly dropped down onto a stool, which creaked under her weight. "We wouldn't know where to begin, and without Jeffrey, we'd be slaughtered by the cultists."

"Hey!" Charlie objected, flexing his biceps and sounding slighted.

"Really?" Kelly asked, doubtfully.

"Okay, no." Charlie dropped his pose and quickly sat down. Kelly chuckled a little and punched her brother in the arm. He feigned injury and stuck out his lip.

Gloria began to cry. Real tears rolled down her cheeks, and she hugged herself, rocking back and forth on her stool. "Oh, no," she said over and over softly.

"Mom." Charlie slid down onto his knees in front of Gloria. "What is it? It's going to be okay, Mom. It's going to be okay. You'll see."

"No, it's not." She blubbered back, tears blurring her words. "Nothing is okay, and now the book…it's over. We're lost. All is lost."

"C'mon, Mom. It's not that bad," Kelly pleaded. "Charlie will win the race, and everything's going to go back to normal."

Gloria sucked in a few tears and looked hard at Charlie. She seemed to appraise him and then finding him wanting began to wail, tears more free-flowing than before.

Charlie knew what she had been thinking, or at least he thought he did. He pulled back from her and began to fear a little. Doubt crept into his mind. *I'm no good. I've always been screwing things up.* He heard his own voice say in his mind. And then he started to believe it.

Kelly watched Charlie fall back. She saw her mother, whose pride and misplaced courage had been passed to Jackie, crumbling. She said aloud, "I wish Jackie was here. Oh, God, help us!"

A voice in her mind that could have been her own said, *What'd you expect, girl? This ain't no party. You don't belong here.* And then seemingly as an afterthought, *What would Jackie do anyway? She's no better than you. What could she do?*

But that was a mistake. It was a mistake because Kelly knew Jackie had said as much. Jackie had never claimed to be better, not a better person, or a better Christian. Second, it was a mistake because Kelly knew exactly what Jackie would do.

When Kelly realized she was being affected by an evil spirit, she felt a chill like it was a giant spider. She shimmied all around trying to wipe herself off and then at last froze with her palms toward the ground. She tightened all her muscles in an attempt to hold still. Then softly, angrily, she said, "Get off me."

Immediately, she felt a little better. "Leave me alone," she commanded more boldly. She felt better still. She relaxed her muscles and shouted, "Be gone!"

Her mind clear, she moved to Charlie and touched him on the shoulder. "Be gone!" she said loudly and firmly and then moved onto to Gloria fully confident that it had worked without waiting for the result. When she knelt next to Gloria, she laid her hands on her mother's now, fetal-positioned form.

"Be gone!" Kelly said, but this time for some unknown reason, she doubted, and nothing seemed to happen. Then Charlie was next to her. He laid his hands on Gloria.

"Evil spirit?" he asked Kelly softly.

"Yep," Kelly said. She was not afraid now. She opened her eyes, and brother and sister met in a knowing glance.

"Be gone!" they commanded together, and at that, Gloria visibly relaxed. They helped her sit up.

"Mom," Kelly said, "You need Christ. Without him, you're not safe. Believe in Jesus, Mom, please."

"Okay, okay, I'm listening." And she listened.

Each time Jackie and Jeffrey mounted on Coal, they watched the world around them disappear and return with new surroundings. They expected to see Kerromyer mansion. Time and again they were disappointed. On the way there, Coal had seemed to disappear above the garden and reappear thousands of miles away over the Middle East. But on the way back, things had changed. He kept dropping in on random places. At each place, he would stand perfectly still until Jeffrey and Jackie dismounted and looked around.

In every case, they found someone about to be slain by some disaster. They were able to move the people away. Apparently, Coal had been watching in Jerusalem when they had saved the crowd from the explosion. He so liked the idea; he thought he would take it to the next level.

As Jackie hauled hard on a car door to free a victim, she looked up at Jeffrey and said, "How long do you think this will go on? This makes seven stops already?"

"I don't know, but I get it. I mean, if the world goes back to whatever it was doing before all this began, these people die. We are like their guardian angels," Jeffrey answered, shutting the car door on his side.

"But the world over? I mean, how many people could be about to die in an instant in the world? Could be a lot."

"The real question is, whether your mom and the others are okay and the kids..." Jeffrey started to feel a bit angry about the delay. When they mounted up again, he told Coal that they needed to get back, and that this was the last stop to save people. That left him wondering how many more people they could have saved.

Coal stopped once more at a gun shop where Jeffrey helped himself to several additional weapons. He tried to convince Jackie to take a machete or a hunting knife but she would not. The image of that demon's smiling face, she didn't know Saul's name, flashed in her memory.

"I don't think we should be killing the bad guys," she said thoughtfully. "Or stealing..." She added the last as an afterthought when Jeffrey slung the rifle up onto his shoulder.

"I hear you," Jeffrey said. "I promise, if I survive this whole thing, I'll pay for everything. I promise."

"Okay."

"As for killing the bad guys, that seems to be more up to them than me. Ya' know what I mean?" His tone was sympathetic but firm.

"I guess so." She thought about whether the cultists would be persuaded. Inside she was angry. She was upset that the cultists were helping the demons, and yet something in her wanted to have compassion on them. She wondered who she had become. She was very pleased with the new her but also a little baffled.

Just then, before they mounted back up the last time, she pulled the now cooled cross from her pocket and put it around his neck.

"For good luck?" he asked. She frowned and turned toward Coal. "What?" he asked. She didn't answer. Everyone had placed some portion of their hopes on retrieving the cross, which had now been done. And now, she was more certain than ever that it meant nothing. She thought about telling Jeffrey but knew he wouldn't like it. So she spent the remainder of the ride praying and formulating what she would say to the cultists if she got the chance.

She had to carry the rifle while they rode because it was stabbing her in the leg, and carrying it made her feel even more uncomfortable than when it had been stabbing her in the leg. Jeffrey was downright pleased and seemed confident. Great contrast separated them as Kerromyer mansion finally came into sight.

———

Saul flew high over the garden, flipped through the pages of the book, and then out of disgust, threw it down into the garden. Useless! He found himself a high perch to think out his next move. There had been a demon there talking to the quarry. He hadn't sent the demon but capitalized on the distraction. So if he hadn't sent the demon, who had? Maybe there were more than two lords vying for control. Since Satan, no other had ever had power like he and Nero. Who could it be?

A melody came to his lips, and he felt calmer. It was almost time anyway. The age of the contest drew very near. All would be underway soon. One thing he knew for sure, he did not want to go down in history as the one who missed this time. Something caught his eye, and he flew off to check it out, a quick distraction before the real event.

31

It Is Time:
The Age of Contest Begins

Nero slumped deep into the overstuffed, leather chair. His bestial form filled every inch of the open space at the center of the chair, which had been moved to directly in front of the fireplace. Tiny glowing embers popped or drifted from the roaring fire and bounced off his leathery legs intermittently.

The dancing flames combined with the strong liquor made his mind swim. His eyes were glazed over slightly. He was enjoying himself so much that he lost track of where he was and what he was up to, and that was a welcome relief to centuries of guerilla warfare.

"Master," A voice from behind him called. Nero noticed a bit of firmness in the call as if it had not been the first, and the caller had been trying to get his attention. The call was a little too authoritative for his liking, but he let it slip as he shook his head and pulled himself a little higher in the chair.

"Yes," Nero answered.

"It's time." His voice shook, and then he rumbled his throat, and it returned clear. "The riders have been chosen and are ready to meet you as you requested."

Nero never looked up but responded, "Where is Saul?"

"I'm sorry, my lord. I do not know."

"Tell them I will be there shortly." The lesser demon left the room.

Nero peered deeply into the fire. He remembered humans burning and screaming in a city long ago. He could see frantic scrambling as ancient technologies were brought to bear against one of the most ancient of destroyers—fire. Water delivered by aqueducts was only available to the parts of the city that did not burn. The wealthy let the poor burn to protect themselves and their property. This was Nero's greatest masterpiece, and it was painted on his memory for all time.

Manipulating the human emperor had been all too easy. Even the young churches had played into his hands by being secretive and thus attracting the hatred of the general populace. It was the beginning of his promotion. He had made his mark on the spirit war. Of course, he had stuck with the emperor for some time after that—motivating him to blame the fire on the Christians and launching the greatest persecution of all time.

Not long after, he met Saul. Saul had manifested long before and had always resented Nero's promotion, but Nero was good at killing Christians and stopping the spread of God's lies among the heathen, and that was what Saul wanted.

Saul had lost control of a situation with a powerful figure he'd been manipulating and was really on the outs. Lots of things Saul had done had not worked out. He'd had the perfect opportunity way back to destroy a man after God's own heart when there were few of those around. That would have really been something.

Somehow Beelzebub had considered that a great victory, even though the human Saul was manipulating, missed from no more than fifteen feet away. Out of that, Saul had been manifested when Nero was still just a lesser influence.

Now Saul was not around when they were about to score their greatest and perhaps final victory. It gave Nero an uneasy feeling. Would Saul make a move to steal away the victory somehow, or would he mess it up? Well, there was nothing for it now. He lingered watching the mental images a few breaths longer and then pushed himself up out of the chair, switching to his well-dressed human form. "It is time," he said through disappearing fangs.

Nero stood behind a small podium, a miniature of one that had been set up on the grass, near the finish line of the track in the arena. He placed both hands on the edges of the podium and surveyed the gathered troops. Behind him, crowds of cultists and demons were pouring into the arena. A few filtered off to hear what he would say.

Gathered before him were ten riders. They were dressed in all kinds of garb. Their nightmares were not present. The nightmares would be in the prep area near the starting gate. Demon riders surrounded the crowd of human riders. All were dressed in jockey habits, and only the pronounced facial bones gave the demon riders away as nonhuman. The demon riders showed no emotion at all as Nero stepped up, which probably meant they were still seething over their displacement. They held their expressions in check in order to hide this fact.

Nero cleared his throat, and then with a great deal of volume said, "We are on the verge of the greatest victory of all eternity! The Age of Contest has begun. Your prowess has brought you here. You are the best riders in the world. Now you will ride for our victory!"

The cultists howled and cheered. Their cries were no great volume as there were only ten of them, but when Nero glared at the demon riders, they added their howls, and the small platform upon which the podium stood shook.

"You are great and mighty warriors each and every one!" He shouted above the din, which brought them to quiet again. "You will crush the human! He is nothing! He is feeble! He is one, and you are many! Will you crush him?"

"We will crush him!" Their cry was not in unison, but it seemed genuine enough.

"Who is the winner?" Nero asked.

"I am!" One rider shouted, and several around him pointed or just looked in his direction.

"Any who aid this man in winning will be rewarded equally. He is our champion! This is our victory! Defeat is not an option!" On the last, he let his hideous demon face show through slightly and hissed the words so that every human ear within range of the sound would be pricked with pain a bit.

"Now," Nero began again. However, this time, he was interrupted as Jackie's dead body crashed into the scene, bouncing off the little platform and flopped to a stop in front of the riders.

There was no gasp as their might be in a crowd of ordinaries. All present took it to be a part of the show, and Nero, looking up to see Saul swooping in from above, decided to act quickly.

"Worse than this to the man who fails me! This is the Christian woman who dared resist us! Now she lies dead at your feet! A fitting place for all who resist the coming of our kingdom!" As Nero finished his roaring, Saul landed beside him.

"She did not have it," Saul said softly. "There is another."

Nero nodded, knowing the implications of another Christian. They would have to go forward with the cultists riding. They could not risk the Christian intervening in the race. It was strictly forbidden, of course. No one from outside the race could aid or detract from any rider's efforts. However, Nero knew that God could not be trusted, and those who worked with him would be no better.

"Have you seen it?' Nero asked softly, while smiling at the riders and assembled onlookers. While they howled and cheered, they had no idea what was unfolding before them.

"No," Saul answered, and it was right in that second that he decided not to tell Nero about the scar. Saul knew the artifact had caused the burn, and that the artifact was round and its approximate size, but that was information that might come in handy at a particular juncture. Nero did not need to know just now.

The little gathering ended. The riders went to stand near their nightmares. They found Charlie already there, his face tear-stained, his jaw firmly set. He stood ready to race.

The other nightmares stayed out of reach of Coal. Their masters' hatred affected them, but Coal was their equal in every way, and they were afraid of him. When the race began, they would be more afraid of losing, but for now, they remained at a distance.

32

Contest!

The Age of Contest had clearly begun. The stands filled with cultists. A cultist band and a troop of cultist crossbowman mustered near where Nero had ordered his throne placed, several rows above the finish line. Hundreds of demons were present as well. Most looked like humans, but one in ten made no attempt to hide their bestial nature. When Nero took his throne, all grew quiet. From then on, you could see lesser spirits soaring everywhere. They had been given lesser manifestation on the edge of this great victory. They appeared as wisps of mist or streaming light and darted this way and that.

The predawn light had not changed, but somehow the spirits and the clouds combined to create a slight strobe effect across the track and field. Any given spot was dancing in and out of feint shadow with every passing breath. The stage was set. The display would be breathtakingly beautiful if the inferences were not so deadly.

Nero and Saul sat, and Nero's hand went up to the chain as the last of the riders, now mounted, settled into the starting gate. When he pulled the chain, the gates would open; and four laps later, the winner would determine the fate of mankind.

Smugly, Nero delayed and looked at Saul as if in mock seeking permission. Then something completely unexpected happened. Kelly stepped up to the podium on the platform at the center of the arena.

The noise of thousands of unruly cultists and chatty demons cancelled out whatever Kelly was saying at first. Then she began to yell one word loudly over and over. Slowly but steadily, silence rippled through the whole stadium. It started with the demons who were making the greatest shrieking and howling but fell silent as they heard her yell. The cultists might have continued but most somehow figured if the demons were silent, they should be also.

Kelly yelled, "Silence," one last time. Nero wasn't even speaking, and he felt compelled to be quiet. *Christian!* he thought quietly.

Kelly began again. "There is something you must know!" Her voice seemed supernaturally amplified, and everyone in the stadium heard her clearly. "There is something you must know!"

Kill her! Nero thought, but he could not bring himself to yell the command. Just then, one of the commanders on the field caught sight of Nero, and he motioned for him to attack. The demon leapt into action, charging the platform. Several armed cultists joined him as did a few other demons.

The demon commander hit the steps shrugging off his human-looking form as he took the platform. His fangs were colored yellow, and his knees were permanently bent at a forty-five degree angle. He had hooves instead of feet. He came quietly but in great haste.

Kelly raised both hands like a traffic officer stopping traffic cars. "Stop! Leave me alone!" she commanded and did not watch as the demons left the ranks of those charging and took up positions fifty to sixty feet from Kelly in several directions. Since they had been leading, their disappearance gave Kelly some breathing room. "I am not your enemy!" she yelled at the charging cultists.

As the first cultist hit the top step, his head exploded, and a portion of the platform began desperately to need a mop. The lead cultist on the stairs on the end of the platform suddenly clutched his chest and fell backward. The report of a rifle fired somewhere far away drifted into the stadium, but it was not until the third or fourth shot and the delayed sound effect that onlookers began to realize that someone was shooting the cultists.

Five cultists were down, and the rest had taken cover at the edge of the platform or behind some nearby bushes. Taking initiative, a commander of the demon riders leapt into the saddle; and though he was still compelled to silence, his example spurred his fellow demon riders to action. Three cultists who rode nightmares but had not made the race also mounted, and thirteen nightmares left the ground in pursuit of the shooter.

Meanwhile, Kelly began her speech again. "You have been deceived. You are potentially in the last moments of your life. If Nero wins, he and his fellow demons will kill you all. They want nothing more than to see the death of all mankind. It is because we can do something that they can't!"

She was twisting in her spot, and her voice projected into the stands. She was even meeting the eyes of any who were not afraid to look at her. She was praying in her heart as she put forth the speech that had been written in her sister's handwriting. She did not know when it had been written, but she knew it had been written for right now.

"Saul killed my sister!" she improvised. "I would like nothing more than to get revenge on him, but I don't have to because I have something that he can never have!"

As she was speaking, a small army of demons had moved from the stands and gathered with the demons she had repulsed by her command. It occurred to her that she had repulsed the whole place. They were all compelled to leave her alone. She actually thought, *Wow, that's awesome,* before turning back to the notes.

"Even now, it is not too late! You can still have what they cannot have. You can be more than they can ever be. They may appear to have power, but look at them, they cannot even touch me! It is because of Christ in me! Even here, on their track, in the Moment, I am safe from them."

It was then that Nero realized that some of the cultists were listening to what she was saying. His heart skipped a beat. *This could not be happening! Could she win souls in the Moment? Could they lose this after all?* He ordered the crossbowmen to open fire by smacking a nearby officer in the back of the head and pointing. A little over half of the troop began readying their weapons and taking aim.

As he returned to his seat, he looked up to see Saul's hand on the chain. Saul had a question on his face. Nero nodded, and the gates opened, and the nightmares shot out onto the track. Charlie shot out to an early lead just as Gloria had instructed him.

Kelly continued to preach, explaining how every person who had ever lived had been separated from God because of their sin and how God had made a way through Jesus to bridge that gap. The crossbowmen took aim, and after three fell to sniper fire, about ten fired at Kelly. She ignored the bolts, even the one that passed through her hair and continued imploring the cultists to listen and be saved.

At the first turn, the riders were stretched out no more than two wide with Coal carrying Charlie easily three lengths in the lead. Charlie wasn't pressing hard. He looked like he could have pulled away but was restraining Coal until someone from the pack made a move. At the halfway point on the first lap, the lead was stretched out to four lengths, and the pack had thinned to one wide with the scheduled winner fourth.

"Jackie is dead, true. I may die here today, true. But if I die, I will go to be with God! I am saved from being eternally separated. What about you? It's a gift from God! It's a gift that you have been deceived into ignoring. God is offering you a pardon! Nero is offering you death and eternal separation. One is a good deal! One is not!"

At the second turn, the pack separated into two groups with the scheduled leader in the middle of the first one. Some of the riders could not keep up. One broke stride and pulled over to the side of the track. Charlie didn't know about him. Another slowed up substantially, apparently having the same idea as the first but being unwilling to act so decisively. Charlie was still three and a half lengths in front of the front pack and managing Coal's exertion. That's how it remained as they passed the finish line the first time. Kelly smiled.

"The time is now!" she yelled. "Just believe on the Lord Jesus Christ and be saved!" The crossbowmen fired, though this time it was only four shots since three more had gone down to sniper fire, and most of the rest were hiding, fearing the sniper fire too much to get up and aim. A few were listening and contemplating what Kelly was saying. One of the four shots actually grazed her shoulder, and she winced but continued to twist and search out with her eyes those that seemed to be affected by her words.

Just then, the demon riders on nightmares engaged the sniper. Jeffrey was bracing from behind a table turned on its side on the twenty-seventh floor of the ripped open skyscraper. The last two volleys of shots, though they had been very telling down below allowed the riders to pick out his position, and they turned toward him as one. All thirteen riders, almost in a line, headed for the opening. The three cultists had spears, and as they neared the twenty-seventh floor, they raised them overhead, prepared to throw them or to jab with them.

From behind a second table back and to Jeffrey's left, Gloria stood and yelled at the demon riders. "Be gone!" she yelled. "Leave us alone!"

Every one of them hated it, and every one of them obeyed. All three cultists threw their spears. Jeffrey fired three shots in rapid succession. The three cultists fell from their saddles, marking the end of the onslaught. One of the spears hit Gloria in the thigh.

Gloria caved backward but did not lose consciousness. She pushed the spear out of her leg and began wrapping it with a scrap of cloth. She could hear the report of the rifle, and she peaked around to make sure they were not in direct danger. No, Jeffrey was firing at the scene below again. One more shot and the rifle clicked a dull empty chamber.

As Jeffrey grabbed another clip and ejected the first, he turned around. "Kids okay?" he asked.

Gloria pulled a blanket back slightly behind the table and saw Jacob and Buddy curled up their sleeping as if nothing was going on around them. The nearest spear had been the one that hit Gloria. The children were fine.

As Charlie came out of the first turn of the second lap, the rider who had broken stride kicked his nightmare to get up to speed and then merged in on Charlie and Coal. He pulled up right along side and took a swing at Charlie with what looked like a large bread knife.

Fortunately, Gloria had prepared him for just this case. Charlie leaned left in the saddle toward the rail but only for a split second. Then as the knife passed and the rider was trying to recover from the force of his own swing, Charlie reined Coal right in front of the other rider. At the same time, he struck out with his right arm and shoved up on the assailant's armpit. The assailant careened off the back of his nightmare and into the path of the oncoming riders. He disappeared in a burst of fire and dust when the first hoof struck. The riders surged forward as if nothing had happened.

Charlie encouraged Coal to pick up the pace a little bit as dealing with the assailant had cut his lead to two lengths. By the second turn of the second lap, he'd made the lead back to three, but he'd also spotted the other rider he was about to lap. The enemy was racing in the outside third of the track and already matching Charlie's pace fairly closely.

As they crossed the finish line beginning the third lap, Charlie heard Kelly yelling for the cultists who were accepting Christ to get out of their seat and to come down to the platform. Out of the corner of his eye, he saw some of the cultists making their way to the aisle. There was some scuffling in the stands as cultist turned against cultist in disagreement over what Kelly was saying.

Meanwhile, Charlie exchanged blows with the enemy rider. The cultist dropped his knife after the first strike but kept swinging. Charlie tried the push maneuver but failed. As they rounded turn two, he could hear the thunderous nightmare hooves behind him growing nearer. The cultist punched him hard in the knee, and Charlie swung wildly breaking the guy's nose.

The lead was gone. The pack was right on Charlie now, and the scheduled winner was coming up on the inside. If he made it up parallel, Charlie would be pinched and could not deflect attacks from both sides unless he let go of the reigns. He leaned forward to encourage Coal and incidentally ducked a wild swing.

"Go, Coal!" Charlie yelled. The flames on Coal's hooves returned, and his speed increased by 50 percent. With only a slight delay, all of the other nightmares caught fire and sped to keep up with Coal.

The shaken assailant fell off until at least the next pass, and the would-be winner dropped off two lengths because it had taken him that long to activate his nightmare's special ability.

No small number of cultists had pushed free from the stands, even overcoming opposition to do so. They began to flock around the platform as the race entered its final lap. A hundred or more cultists stared boldly up at all the demons and cultists that remained above them, for the first time in freedom.

The converted cultists were under attack however. Many cultists began to gather around the converted cultists and throw insults and in some cases, weapons at them. They defended themselves however they could but stayed together, and their numbers were actually swelling even as some were falling to the attacks.

Jeffrey was reloading again when lesser spirits entered their makeshift base and began to circle them. A white swirl and a greenish colored one tried to wrap around Jeffrey. He ignored them. Gloria shouted at them to leave and they did. As Jeffrey fired several more shots down into the scene below, both crosses fell from his shirt. They dangled on the end of their chains; the longer chain was the cross of the martyr retrieved from Jerusalem. The shorter chain held Jackie's cross. She had placed it in his hand with her dying action. He'd already committed in himself that he'd probably never take it off though he noted it would need to be scrubbed having some of her blood still in the cracks.

Even as the troops were gathering around her, Kelly continued to preach and exhort more response. At that, a flabbergasted Nero had enough. He turned to Saul and motioned to Kelly and drew a line with one finger across his neck. He knew Saul would understand. In fact, was surprised Saul had waited this long.

Nero went back to taking stock of the situation. Three riders were very close together, vying for the lead on the backstretch of this, the last lap. It could be anyone's race.

That was better than last count but still not good enough. "She must have the item," he croaked. "Kill her and get it."

A shiver went down Nero's spine, and he shed his human-looking appearance but too late. Saul wrapped his giant fist around Nero's throat, which enlarged even as he clutched it. With the strength of ages, Saul hoisted the surprised and flailing Nero into the air and threw him over the rail, down to the bottom of the steps that lead under the bleachers.

Full blown conflict threatened to erupt between the converted or converting cultists and the others. Jeffrey picked off a few unconverted crossbowmen who dared to show their heads. With fire erupting from his hooves, Coal raced to the finish line with two other contenders hot on his tale, neither even a length behind.

Saul leapt from the rail and dropped the thirty feet intending to land on Nero, but Nero was ready and sent Saul flying with a grasp and a kick of both feet. Saul flew through one of the metal support beams, and that section of the stands immediately groaned. His butt carved a small trench in the ground, but all the while, he retained the grasp on his spear.

Nero approached Saul confidently. "I knew it would come to this." Nero hissed.

"Always had to," Saul said as he sprang to his feet. Nero tried to rush in but couldn't make it before Saul was ready with the spear. "Now, whatever happens, I'm gonna end you."

"Not likely," Nero responded. "And when we finally win it all, you will have missed it once again."

"We are beaten except next time, it will be me that faces them. I will be in charge!"

Nero made a move, and as Saul thrust the spear, he grabbed it and yanked hard. Saul dug his talon feet into packed gravel and pulled. Two eight-foot tall demons in a tug of war over a spear…

Then suddenly, Saul lashed out with his clawed hand and put out Nero's eye. Nero staggered back and let go of the spear. Saul jumped forward and body slammed him to the ground. He knelt on the chest of his former leader with the spear raised, clenched by the shaft, with both hands. "It's over," Saul said.

At that same instant, the unconverted cultists who outnumbered the converted ones ten to one, surged. A battled ensued. If the race had gone on another lap, it would have been blocked by the rolling melee.

Charlie crossed the finish line. He crossed it half a length ahead of the next nearest rider. He crossed the finish line and won. He won and before everyone could wonder what would happen next, the Moment was over.

33

Paladins and Publishing

In the room that had been Charlie's office, Jeffrey sat writing by the light of an old, dim oil lamp. The shade of the lamp was soot covered, but it still burned brightly enough to see clearly in the little room. Jeffrey picked up the book and strode to the door. He opened it and met a man outside. The two walked very solemnly to the great room where a meeting of men like Jeffrey was already underway. The paladins sat around a large square of tables, and Jeffrey walked to in front of the head man. He placed the book there and then took a seat in an open chair next to him.

The head man took up his glass and stood tall. "A toast," he called and all the men rose to their feet. "A toast." Then when they were all standing with glasses upraised, Jeffrey included, he said, "To being ready!" They repeated the phrase and all drank. It was the first of many such toasts, and Jeffrey would regale them with tails of his experiences. The mansion was a museum during the day, and Buddy was fine and in a good private school, but just then, he was away on a vacation trip with some friends.

—⁓—

The sun burned hot in the sky, and Kelly was slathering on some more lotion as the children played in the surf with Charlie. Gloria was flipping through the final pages of an eight-and-a-half-by-eleven manuscript. They lounged on beach chairs, and a beach house was in the background. Out to sea some distance, two men were racing across a fairly calm ocean on sailboards.

"I took some creative license," Kelly said. "But what do you think?"

"It's wonderful. I mean, I've always heard it said that fact is often stranger than fiction. In this case, I hope God can use it. I mean I know he can. It's just that…"

"What?" Kelly asked as a flock of seagulls swooped lazily overhead. Before Gloria could answer, some seagull poop appeared with a slap on Kelly's foot. "Really?" she blurted. She frantically wiped the poop in the sand before turning back to Gloria.

"It's just that…" Gloria began and then seemed to be trying to put it delicately, "How do you know that anyone will publish it? It isn't that easy to get started with writing especially with such a fantastic tale."

"Oh," Kelly began with a chuckle. "I've taken care of that." She produced a card from her beach bag. Gloria flipped the card over and read Kelly's name and her title, President. The business name was Coal Publishing. "I bought a publishing house."

The two of them laughed until they got up and went to play in the surf.

———∿∿∿———

Broadby's books was always hopping on Friday nights. The clerks looked with concern at the man in a pinstriped suit with an eye patch and sunglasses. It had been dark for half an hour.

Still, he didn't need help and found the section with relative ease. Christian fiction. The book was *Blood Bowl* by Kelly Kerromyer. The strange man paid the purchase price and tax without saying a word. He left his receipt behind. The cover of the book had a sunrise and a ripped open skyscraper on it. A little gold seal indicated it had spent three weeks on *The New York* Times best seller list as of that printing.

The man in the pinstriped suit sat down on a green-painted, slightly peeling park bench and began to skim through. Just as he found the chapter he was looking for, a scrawny, chisel-beaked teenager in thin-rimmed glasses, a short-sleeved shirt with a pocket protector and several pens in it sat down next to him. The teen said nothing while he read but fidgeted a lot.

One page after another, the man read. He seemed riveted. He flipped page after page, and though the chapter was fairly short, he grimaced several times. When he was through, he set the book down on his thigh in one hand with his finger in his page. Silently, his mouth rounded the word, "Bowl."

"That Kelly Kerromeyer, she's really hot, huh?" the scrawny teen asked. "And it's a really good book, huh? Been on the best seller's list a real long time now."

The man's face deepened in color as the teen talked, but the scrawny teen continued, oblivious. He searched into the parking lot, waiting for a ride. The man sat up straighter.

"Ya know what's amazing?" the teen asked. "I think a lot of what's in there could actually be true. Ya know what I mean? How do we know stuff like that doesn't really happen? As for me, I been thinking about getting in church, ya know? And getting ready just in case, ya know?" As he stopped talking, he looked the man in the face for the first time and saw himself reflected in mirrored shades. He swallowed hard.

Seconds later, the bestial form of Nero soared off into the night. In his left hand, he clutched the book. With his right hand, he crushed and dropped a pair of wire-rimmed glasses spattered in something red. They fell near the empty

park bench.

AFTERWORD

Mysteries Revealed

There are a lot of things we do not know about the universe. You could spend a lifetime exploring whatever little corner of it you are given access to and learn so little as to be negligible. On the other hand, truth is not relative, and so it is possible to know some things. These facts can then be acted on to determine others and science, which was meant essentially to be an exploration of our environment, gets its birthing. This hopefully entertaining tale may or may not sell. It may wind up in the fantasy section of the local bookstore, in the Christian fiction, or even science fiction section. However, many aspects of this book are very real.

I'd like to clear that up a bit if I may.

As far as we know, the Moment is not a real event. That probably does not strike you as a surprise. The characters in the book are not real and are not based on any living person.

However, demons are real and are nothing to be trifled with. Evil spirits are real and may have some of the described effects. It is almost certain that historical figures such as Nero, emperor of Rome, Saul, first king of Israel, Saul Christian persecutor, or Esau, brother of Jacob, were indeed influenced by evil spirits to undertake some of the evil acts that they were known for. Indeed, the Bible says that an evil spirit was plaguing Saul, the first king of Israel. Only the music of David could soothe him. Jesus cast out demons and evil spirits of various kinds and gave the disciples the same ability.

The Bible is real. You can buy one at the same literary outlet where this book came from. People debate how much of it is actually authoritative, but I would like to say to you that I believe the Bible 100 percent.

Followers of Jesus do have authority in the spiritual realm and possess some ability, by the Holy Spirit and God's grace, to rebuke evil spirits and demons. The chief of the demons was Satan, and though he was probably once an angel, he is a rebel against God, a deceiver (with much practice) and will be separated from God for eternity. In the mean time, he continues his fight, with the help of his allies, as if he had not lost. It seems that the supreme deception Satan has perpetrated, he has actually perpetrated on himself. He has convinced himself that God is not good, or that evil will somehow triumph.

The whole story of the universe is the story of God reconciling men to himself through Jesus Christ, his son. John 3:16 Everything, and I mean everything that goes on has something to do with this struggle. God and his side try to make peace with those who have yet to understand. Satan and his side try to see to it that the message is sufficiently confused so that people will not come to the realization that what they really need is a relationship with God. Matthew 24:4

I can, by no means, explain the mysteries of the universe in these short pages. However, I felt compelled to tell every reader that the salvation that is pictured here is actually available. All people have made mistakes, and these mistakes (intentional or otherwise) have separated them from God. Romans 3:23; 6:23a God sent Jesus to pay the price so that a person might find their way to God. Romans 6:23b Basically, it's a totally free gift, already paid for by God. Ephesians 2:8 If you try to pay for it, you cannot have it. Ephesians 2:9 You'll get something for your labor, but it will not be salvation. Matthew 11:28

So we all mess up. Messing up yields separation from God. If that separation is not mended then, when the time comes, when God renews the whole universe and there are only two places left, with him or away from him, then we would be away from him. Matthew 7:23

The good news is, even though the wages of our wrong-doing is death (eternal separation), the gift of God is eternal life through Jesus Christ, his son. Romans 6:23 God wants to save us. Indeed, there is only one Lord of the universe and one rebel cause, and every person is on one side or the other in every moment.

Just ask God to save you through Jesus Christ, his son, and you will never be put to shame. Romans 10:13 Mean it though; it's not a magic formula. You have to actually be willing, and he promises he will do it. When you decide this, you are getting a fresh start. John 3:3 You can pretty much forget everything that went on before because all old things are passed away now, and everything in your life is made new. 2 Corinthians 5:17

Starting over fresh in Jesus is often called being born again and is described in John 3 among other places.

Before, after, and during your walk with Christ, you will still have to deal with evil spirits and demons because they have a strong presence on earth. 1 John 4:1 The good news is, God is stronger than they are by far. Not by virtue of who you are but by virtue of who Christ is in you, you will be given authority to overcome these things. 1 John 4:4

I think there is wisdom in not engaging evil spirits of any kind in conversation. They are crafty, and there will always be a part of you that seeks a shortcut to knowledge—Eve's problem (Genesis 3.) So listen only to God. Seek more knowledge about him, read a Bible, and think about what you are supposed to be. Get involved in a Bible-teaching or Bible-preaching church. Get baptized. Talk to your pastor about this once you find a church and inform them of your decision to follow Christ. Matthew 10:32

The truth about God is not fiction. That is the effort of evil to keep people from believing and being saved. God loves you, and if you will give these things a fair hearing, then I know that you will find a need of him inside you. Don't settle for any imitation. Make sure that you are following the God of the Bible only. This can be accomplished only through Jesus. If you do it through him, then you can't get it wrong. John 16:33

If you need more answers before you get started on your walk with Christ, then get to a church near you. Do realize that some Christians have been misled by evil spirits because they entered into conversation with them somehow, and so you really need a church that teaches the

Bible. You will ultimately be responsible for yourself when the time comes, so you need to get used to asking the hard questions and getting the answers. Psalm 119:11, James 1:5

Study, pray, love others, tell others what you know to be true, and spend time with other believers for starters. Then learn to test everything by what the Bible says about it, and you can become a productive disciple of Jesus.

If all this sounds like a lot, just tell God you are trusting in Jesus today. Tell him you are sorry you screwed up, and you are willing to accept his forgiveness and leadership and then see what comes next. Romans 10:9–10

Lastly, I wouldn't put it off. Settle it right now. Jesus said that there would be a lot of folks to hear this message and have it snatched away from them by Satan and his cronies before the message could take root. So get right with God today, and then you know that when the time comes, you are ready.

EPILOGUE

Going Home

That's when Jackie figured it out. When we described the demon, she remembered him from the first real encounter in the garden. She said he'd grabbed Jeffrey, and that she'd had to order him off. She said she'd ordered him to show the way to the children, but the thing had just up and flew away immediately after that. Then she really got excited because she said she had remembered seeing him later too. She had seen him standing on the semitrailer on the grounds.

"I'll bet that's where they have the children," Mom had said.

"Sounds good," Jeffrey had said and before long we were on our way. We were ready for the Age of Contest except it seems they weren't ready for us. Jeffrey had thought, with having to fly all the way across the world, we'd have been running behind, but when we checked by the stadium where the race would be, we saw no one there. Even the races from before were not going on.

We crept to the semitrailer. The demon was not there, at least not in view. We passed traffic overgrown with weeds and creepy flowers from the garden. One man sat perfectly still in the driver's seat of his shiny little compact car with vines wrapped over his arms and around his head. The image was bizarre and a little unnerving.

As we snuck up to the back of the truck, we could see two men guarding the doors, which were closed tight. They seemed to be human or otherwise very good replicas. They were dressed in modern gang colors, and their pants sagged down low.

Charlie and Jackie slipped to the right, and Jeffrey worked his way through the hedges to the left after handing me the rifle. Mom and I watched and prayed. We held hands concealed in a little copse of trees. The men stood stark still as if frozen in place. When Charlie and Jeffrey were set, Jackie jumped out in front of the men.

"Freeze!" she commanded. She pointed her empty hand at them as if she were holding a gun. The confused gang members looked at one another, and then one flipped open a knife and the other raised a machete, which had been propped on the back bumper of the truck.

Charlie stepped out on the guy with the knife. The bat sliced through the air ending with a ringing *thud*. The bat slammed full force into the man's forehead. He went down and groaned slightly, indicating he was still alive. Charlie bent over him apologizing.

Jeffrey had lunged from the bushes to grab the machete arm of the other guy. The guy took a swing at Jeffrey with his offhand, and Jeffrey caught it. Holding both hands high above his head, Jeffrey spun the guy around while still wrestling for control of the machete.

Jackie took two quick steps and planted her foot between the guy's legs with all her might. The guy let go of the machete and sagged like his pants. Jackie spun in place and kicked him in the jaw. He slammed into the ground hard.

"Who needs a paladin?" Jeffrey asked as Mom and me were joining them at the back of the trailer.

"I do," Jackie answered, and they met eyes for an instant before turning their full attention to the lock. As we stared at it, Jeffrey produced a key from the bat-to-the-head cultist. Sure enough it fit, and we swung the big doors open wide.

A demon, already in beast form, was waiting just inside the door and attacked before anyone could say anything. He backhanded Charlie with a two-foot long crablike claw. He snarled and leapt forward knocking Mom, Jackie, and me down. Stunned and somewhat breathless, we were delayed in rebuking him.

Another demon in beast form and two cultists in zululike garb arrived at the back of the trailer, and things went from bad to worse. Jeffrey dove into the demon who was standing over us and slid off to the point that he was just wrapping his arms around the thing's thigh.

The demon grabbed Jeffrey in its claw and slung him up and back like a rag doll. The demon coming down off the truck received the pass and slammed Jeffrey into the open door of the truck, which swung all the way around fully slamming open. Since the door moved freely, the blow didn't break bones. Then when the demon threw him at Charlie, he missed and Jeffrey landed in a bush, which wasn't the worst thing that could have happened.

Demon number one lifted Jackie up by the throat, which probably hurt a lot because his hand was a pincer claw. She tried in vain to pull the claw open enough to speak or at least breathe. Meanwhile, his foot was on my chest, and I couldn't get a breath. I croaked out a few consonants, but it wasn't any more of a command than a frog might say.

Demon number two went after mom as the cultists stopped at the edge of the truck. One of the cultists raised his spear, ready to throw, while the other balanced on his heals as if to stand firm against an unseen attacker.

Mom rolled and scrambled, slipping between Jackie and crab-hand demon. Then having caught her breath, she spun and faced them just as demon number two's hairy hand touched her blouse. "Freeze!" she yelled.

The demons looked quizzically at her. For long enough to be terrified, I thought they were going to ignore her and kill us all. Then it became evident that they had stopped moving. The expressions on their faces changed from "I'm going to destroy you," to "I'm going to reluctantly obey you," and everyone breathed a sigh of relief.

The spear grazed mom's shoulder as she ducked away from it in reflex. With that distraction, it seemed like hairy-hand demon was going to grab her, but she spun back on him in an instant and raising one finger, she said, "Ah, ah, ah." Oddly, I could sympathize with what the demon must have been feeling because she used to do that to me about getting another cookie during my childhood.

Three gunshots went off very close to my ear, and I looked right to see that Jeffrey had crawled from the bush and finished the two cultists with his pistol. So much for quiet, but that put an end to the battle, anyway.

"Release them," Mom commanded.

Jackie looked at Mom. "Oh, Mom, Thank God. But when?"

"Yes, and while you were off running around the world dear," Mom answered.

"Wow," Jackie said. She rubbed her neck and shook her head to try to clear the confusion.

Charlie wasted no time. Once he recovered from the crab hand to the face, he climbed into the back of the truck. Jeffrey arrived at about the same time, and Charlie pressed inward while Jeffrey helped the rest of us up. Before she moved to climb up, Mom told the demons to fly to Podunk, Iowa and to speak to no one of what had happened here.

"Is there really such a place as Podunk, Iowa?" Jackie asked Mom as she aided Jeffrey in helping mom into the trailer.

"I'm not sure but who cares anyway," Mom grunted.

The semitrailer was about one-third full with cargo of some kind, crates marked only with a shipping company logo. The cargo didn't concern us. We worked our way deep inside, and there we found Jacob and Buddy comatose but alive.

"Are they drugged?" Jeffrey asked as he entered the little room formed by the crates and the walls of the trailer.

"I don't know," Charlie said. "Looks more like they are just asleep like everyone else."

Jeffrey and I moved to Buddy and Jacob and hugged them long and hard. The rest of us gathered around and with tears from all, we clenched together, happy to be reunited. After what seemed like a long time, someone or maybe everyone realized that we had to get moving.

Jeffrey picked up Buddy, but Charlie stepped up and said he'd better let Charlie carry him so Jeffrey could fight. I carried Jacob, and Jackie led the way out of the trailer with Mom next and Jeffrey quick behind. As we exited the trailer into the predawn light, I was feeling pretty good.

Then as Jackie jumped down and Jeffrey moved up past Mom to go next, we were ambushed. The very large demon we had made the deal with in the garden came from up and behind and shoved an eight-foot spear through Jackie's back. Mom and I screamed. Jeffrey spun and fell on his back, firing the pistol up at the demon, which we hadn't yet seen.

The demon descended on Jeffrey and snatched him by the shoulder. His mighty gray hand dug into flesh. It was clear he was flying and intended to take Jeffrey and get away. Jeffrey was being dragged along the ground as the demon was getting enough air speed to make his escape.

Mom and I were both stunned, but I managed to yell, "Stop!" It worked. The demon pulled up and landed his legs one on either side of Jeffrey. He turned. Jeffrey pulled hard at the fingers of the demon's hand trying to get loose but could not pry them open.

"Let go of him," Mom rebuked.

"I do not think you know what you are saying," the demon began.

"I know exactly what I am saying! Let go of him!" Mom commanded.

"How can you?" the demon asked with an incredulous tone. His words were spit out with a hiss. "You are so young in your faith. You have not learned anything yet." He began to walk slowly forward but had dropped Jeffrey.

Jeffrey immediately scrambled along the ground toward Jackie. She was pierced through the chest, and the first twenty inches of the spear were imbedded in the ground. It was clear she wanted to lie down but could not because the spear was holding her up. I couldn't look at her. My heart was breaking, and my mind was screaming in terror.

"Listen to me for just a few moments," the demon began. "I am Saul. I want to make another deal with you. I will help you in exchange—"

"Shut up!" The exasperated cry came from Jackie just as Jeffrey was helping her lie down.

"You are dying," the demon said. "Soon you will see the fruitlessness of your faith. You will experience firsthand the cruel joke God has played on you."

"I said shut up! Say no more!" Jackie gasped.

"Say no more!" Mom added, seeming to understand only that Jackie wanted it. "Be gone!"

The demon scrunched up his big ugly demon face as if he really wanted to get the last word but was restrained from doing so and then leapt into the air and was gone.

Everyone gathered around Jackie, and Jeffrey cradled her head on his thigh and brushed the hair back from her face. Blood welled up on the insides of her lips. It was like a deep red shadow just behind as she spoke.

"Oh, well, now this sucks," Jackie said.

"You're going to be okay," Jeffrey said.

"Yeah," Jackie answered. "But not in the way you mean."

"It's bad, Jackie," Charlie said. "What do you want us to do?"

"Leave me," Jackie said. "Save the children, win the race, but no matter what, save the children, you get me?" Then she was reaching up toward her neck for something. Mom helped her, and she removed her little silver cross and pressed it, slightly bloody into Jeffrey's hand. "Take this," she said. "Promise me you will think about Jesus."

"I'll think about it," he said and right then while she was still conscious enough to see it, he put the chain around his neck so that Jackie's cross hung next to the one from Jerusalem.

We all told her we loved her, even Jeffrey. Everyone except Jeffrey was crying. The children lay on the ground, oblivious to what was going on a few feet away. She pulled the bowl out from underneath her shirt. Her blood was on it, and it glowed brightly. She shoved it toward me. I took it and pressed it in my belt like she had. In that instant, it seemed almost unimportant.

"The demons," she began. "You can't talk with them. Always tell them to be silent first thing. Do you understand? And they must not get the bowl." As she spoke, some blood spilled from the corner of her mouth. My stomach turned upside down, and I was forced to look away. The blood ran down her chin.

She pressed several rolled up pieces of paper into my hand and overcoming gasping, she said, "It's up to you now. It's up to you. I've got to go home. Going home." Then she fell back, dead.

We lingered a little longer than we should have. Mourning pressed us down I think. But eventually, we left her lying there and snuck back to our stables home away from home. There we found Coal waiting and mom pulled us together to formulate a plan. The papers turned out to be a written out plea to the cultists to recognize their folly in trusting Nero and his demon allies.

Even with all our troubles and rescuing the children, we still had time to spare to get ready for the coming conflict. I will always wonder at what took them so long to be ready.

Though time was technically standing still, we were not and they gave us so much opportunity to prepare.

I practiced my speech in my hiding place under the platform, and Jeffrey and Mom took the kids and the bowl to a safe distance. Charlie brushed down and otherwise prepared Coal. The demons left us alone. The cultists seemed so preoccupied that even when, on the way into the arena, we walked by, a group of them gathered around a platform, they refused to notice us.

With sorrow our companion, we were ready. I remember thinking, *Let's get this over with*. Then the Age of Contest began.